MW01644541

SOMETIMES A LOVE WON'T LET GO

Shima Howard

ISBN 979-8-218-59523-4

*Names have been changed to protect the guilty… IYKYK

Printed in the United States of America

Publisher: Shima Howard

Publisher Consultant: Sophisticated Press

Book Design: Sophisticated Press

www.sophisticatedpress.com

Dedication

This book is dedicated to my son Rico A. Saggus Jr. (#forever22). I would've never known you'd read my manuscript if Quez hadn't asked me when I was gonna finish it. I asked him how did he know about it and he said ma Rico told me about it. He said you was fire with the writing. I'm glad you had the opportunity to read it and see me as human, as a woman and not just as your mom. You are the greatest blessing and gift that came from such an unsavory union. I'm sorry that you departed this life before you could read the final product. I did it for you son. You can rest well knowing that I'm okay. May God continue to own and bless your sweet, sweet soul. I love you so much son, in this life and the next. #LongLiveRico #Ride4Rico #LiveLikeRico

*Honorable mention to my niece Korean (Taie) Bowden who lost her precious beautiful life at the hands of domestic violence 9/9/2011 #LongLiveTaie

Acknowledgment

I would like to honor my Lord and Savior Jesus The Christ for never leaving me. I trust in your promise you have for my life. I know Permissive will leads to Perfect will. You were ALWAYS on time. Thank you! There are a host of people who encouraged me to finish this book. However, I can't name all of you. In no particular order: El, Shan, Rahkia, Angela, Bink, EM, Cookie, Bishop Bickers, Pam, Donna, Beasley, Quez (thanks for providing the tool for me to finish it).

Last but not least my beautiful daughters Niambi and Jameria. Being your mom is the only job I ever loved. God, I thank you for my much-needed inspiration in the form of my granddaughter Ahilan Poole (you are my Sonshine) and my mom Lerlene Bozeman(for all the stories trapped in your head that you never can tell).

Thank you all from the bottom of my heart for your relentless support.

TABLE OF CONTENTS

THE BEGINNING

January 14, 1999

I packed everything I owned (clothes and shoes) and my kids' belongings. Not thinking of the consequences nor weighing the repercussions. In the blink of an eye, my whole life changed. I leave behind a lifestyle of luxury. The ghetto fabulous kind… nice cars and a comfortable home. Whatever I wanted or desired materialistically, I had. Literally, I also left a very abusive, violent, out-of-control supposed fiancé—my everything of 4 years, 5 months, 11 days, 46 minutes, and 22 seconds. My heart is racing, and my mind is blank! What in the hell am I doing? I love him; I'm not supposed to leave. I'm supposed to stick it out. The beatings, the horrible beatings.

My man used to dream shit and commence to whipping my ass. Talking about, I dreamt you were fucking some nigga named Tee, and I was looking at you riding his dick, and you were just smiling at me and laughing at me and shit. So I asked his dumb ass if this was just a dream, why in the hell did you punch me in my face? All he said was he just couldn't imagine any other nigga with his hands all over me, and the look on my face seemed so real. Other than that, he just didn't know and was sorry again, as usual. Disrespectful son of a bitch! That man called me so many bitches and hoes that I started believing it was a part of my given name. He would talk to me like I was nobody. Telling me things like bitch you ain't shit, stank ass ho. Whatever came to mind, he said. He didn't care who was around. All in the same breath, he professed his undying love for me. I felt so small and humiliated. He tried fucking my friends and even my family. He succeeded a few times. While he was sleeping around with hoes, I was "Miss, I got something to prove," standing right by his side.

Too scared to leave. I was too afraid to do anything but stay and pray that he would change and recognize me for the woman I was. You know, smart, loving, kind, gentle, passionate, funny, sexy, thoughtful, sweet, considerate, understanding, brilliant, beautiful, bout it-bout it, sympathetic, ride or die, and as nasty as I needed to be (if you know what I mean)! I was hurt and embarrassed by the things he did and said to me, but I kept grinning and bearing it, all of it. I was expected to take all of the abuse, physical and mental because he takes care of me. What was I doing, leaving all of this behind me? I was saving my life. I didn't want to die! At the same time, I was saving Raheem's life. I wanted to save him from throwing away his music career. Something he'd worked so hard for. He wants to be a music producer. I was saving him from the pain of not being able to raise his children and saving him from being enslaved in the white man's prison for murder. My murder, yes, I thought he would eventually kill me. By the grace of GOD, I can tell my story……………………..

My name is Skylar L. Patterson. The L stands for Love. I was born February 14, 1972, on Valentine's Day, so you know I had to be a sweetie. My mother really didn't want another child, but she didn't believe in abortions. Even though she knew I was coming, I was still an unexpected twist in her already knotted-up life. My mom already had four children—four hot-tailed little girls. Not to mention, it had been 11 years since she had been with child. My oldest sister, Aliyah, was 17 when I was born. She was black as night with teeth so bright, white, and pretty- when she smiled, it looked like you had turned on a flashlight.

I remember her being in the Navy, and when she would come home on a break, she would always have a care package just for me filled with different kinds of hair care products, body lotions, nail polish, clothes, shoes, and perfumes. She also had funny stories she would tell us. Like the time she and her husband had been drinking and smoking weed after he had beat her up for something she didn't clearly remember. So she let him think it was over by getting toasted with him and later fucking his brains loose on their undressed waterbed, which was covered with baby oil. Kinky huh? Once he fell asleep, she tied his hands together with stockings and his feet the same way. Now, anybody who knows anything about stockings knows that you can't untie the knot when it's tied properly. You have to cut them off because the more you struggle the tighter the knots become.

Anyway, she left him lying there asleep. She dressed, packed her bags, and sat them by the door. She called her a cab, lit her another joint, and yelled his name to wake him up. Once he responded, she told him that this was the last time he would ever put his hands on her and not die behind it. She told him she needed to teach him a lesson on how to whoop someone's ass. With that being said, she started beating him with a thick leather belt. With every lash, he screamed and tried to get up. The waterbed was too slippery and in fluid motion, so he was a duck stuck in the mud. She kept smoking and kept beating him with that belt. He had black and blue marks all over his back, ass, thighs, arms, chest, legs and his red ass face. Yeah, he was a high-yellow brother. He kept begging and crying for her to stop, but she didn't stop until she heard her cab blowing his horn outside. Before she left, she told him he had been cruising for a bruising. We all laughed forever about that one.

Emon was 15, small in stature, with a reddish brown Afro. Sweet but sneaky and devious as hell. She once trapped this girl who tried crawling in her bedroom window by closing it on her head. She then proceeded to stick broomstick straws up the girl's nose until she started bleeding. She was terrible, but you wouldn't have known because she was everyone's favorite. Mainly because she was so tiny and could hit flips like professionals had taught her. Everyone thought she would be an Olympic gymnast 'cause that girl could flip her ass off! She still has pictures of herself doing a split on a balance beam in the Mayor's office in Atlanta. The girl was bad! Back then, people thought only little skinny ass, anorexic ass, bulimic ass, Anglo-Saxons could be gymnast.

Phyoncia was 13. Smooth as a fox. Halfway bowlegged, or so she thought. Smart,-cute, and strange as hell. She was always burning a candle or incense. She had people thinking she knew black magic. She would sit on her bedroom floor and put together 1000-piece puzzles in the dark by candlelight. Sneaking out of the house with boys and wearing this fucked up ass powder blue eye shadow that made her look like one of those beauty salon mannequins that cosmetologists experimented on.

Lastly, there was Jewelz. She was 11 and mad as hell at me for being the new baby. She was a cute little bald-headed something. She hated me from the jump. She tried to pull me off the bed when my mom wasn't looking. She pinched me, scratched me, everything and anything she could do and get away with, she did. It was a good thing I went on ahead and grew up cause I didn't stand a chance against the mad girl from hell.

My mom had her tubes cut and burned. Through some act of GOD, her tubes fused back together. After a night of drinking and partying in May of 1971, my dad broke her off something proper and brought me into existence. Still no boy. 5 little girls with different daddies, attitudes, ideas, and feelings about life. I'd say we were pretty much average tho. Like most families that grew up in the hood. Dysfunctional! There's always a mother struggling to support her family, doing what she knows she has to do, and always an absent father, dodging his responsibilities. Which strangely enough leads little girls and grown women alike to lean toward men or significant others as father figures.

I grew up in what a lot of people would call the ghetto. In my eyes, I grew up in the hood. There is a difference. The ghetto is a poverty-stricken community full of crime, drugs, alcohol, and welfare-dependent mothers that can best be compared to criminals with life sentences. Institutionalized! They become so use to their situation that they are now complacent and don't know how to get out. Afraid to try something different other than the norm of what they know. Scared to hope because if they try and fail, they come up with less than they already have. So they settle. Well, I say nothing ventured, nothing gained, but that's just my philosophy.

Now, the hood is the total opposite through my eyes. If someone had told me we were poor, I wouldn't have been able to tell. We had food. It may have been pork & beans and weenies, sandwiches and cereal, or oodles of noodles for a couple of days, but that was normal. We had clothes. I'm talking about good shit. Polo, Tommy, Guess, and who could forget the Jordache jeans, silk shirts, and the belt buckle the size of a small saucer with your picture in it? Whatever was in, we had it. There was always a hustle in the hood, from selling drugs and gambling, to boosters who stole most of that fly shit and came around and sold it in the neighborhood for half price or next to nothing if they were on crack and hard up for a few bucks to get high. We lived in a five-bedroom, two full baths, kitchen, separate living room, dining room 4-level all brick government palatial apartment based on your income. So if you didn't have an income (and some people lied about having jobs just to keep their heads above water), then you didn't have any rent to pay because they didn't have anything to base your income on. You could also find the flyest cars, cutest sistas, and coolest brothas in my hood.

Not to get it twisted, there were some busted and disgusted sistas and brothas around too, who had some beat-up rides. All in all, it still got them from point A to point B. I wouldn't have traded it for the world; I didn't have any other world to compare it too. Thomasville Heights Housing Projects, my home sweet home!

It is late July in the summer of 1995. It's hot, 95 degrees at 12:30 pm, and expected to rise 3 degrees more before 3 pm. The sun is shining so bright it's almost blinding. There is not a hint of a breeze coming any time soon. I guess the air conditioning unit is broken on this bus because all the windows are down, and hot air is gushing in like flames from a fire. It feels like somebody's blow-drying my face. Looking out the window, I somehow get lost in a nostalgic memory of me and Zaye sitting in the house drinking some champagne called Freixenet. We were talking about going to the park for a picnic, but it was so hot outside that day that we figured we would be miserable in all that heat. So we decided it was better to be inside with the AC blowing and drinking some bubbly. It's funny how something so insignificant as burning up in this heat can bring back a memory.

I'm riding the #49 Thomasville bus to Thomasville Housing Projects. Thomasville Elementary School comes into view, and I'm brought back to reality because this is my stop where I get off. I pull the string to ring the bell, signaling the bus to stop, and we slowly pull to the curb so I can get off. It was clear that the bus driver was getting more and more frustrated with me by the way she rolled her eyes and continuously popped the gum she was chewing. I'm struggling trying to get off the bus with a stroller, the baby's bag, my purse, and the baby, and she got the nerve to sit there looking like a moo cow with those ugly crunchy ass basket weave braids, #27 at that. Who still wears the #27 weave? You know that 14kt gold color. That style is so played out. Nobody's trying to help me, and I don't want their damn help 'cause I got this. She's just gonna have to be patient. People kill me accepting jobs in customer service dealing with the public and don't have a humble bone in their body. I can't wait to get a car.

We get off the bus at Henry Thomas Dr. and McDonough Blvd. I hear somebody calling my name as I start pushing Nandi in her stroller down the street, headed toward my sister's apartment. "Hey Skye....hey girl, Skye! What's up, lady?" It's Tela, one of Raheem's friends, trying to get my attention. He was driving a black 1994 Expedition with 22-inch chrome rims. He's blasting "Can You Get Away" by 2 Pac from his Me Against the World album.

"Could it be my destiny to be lonely? Or checking for these hoochies that be on me cause they are phony. With you it's different, I got no need to be suspicious 'cause I can tell my life with you would be delicious.

The way you lick your lips and shake your hips got me addicted. I'm sitting here hoping we can find some way to kick it; tell me, can you get away......so much pressure in the air......and I can't get away I'm unhappy here, all I want to know is you can get away?"

I hear him calling me, but I'm singing along with the song cause that's my jam! He finally pulls up beside me and turns down the music. "Hey girl, my man has been trying to get with you for a minute now. What's up with you? Do you have a man or something? Why don't you want to holla at him?" "Your man ain't said nothing to me. He always got somebody else trying to talk for him. He needs to approach me himself. He acting all shy. He knows damn well he ain't shy," "Girl, you crazy. I'm telling him he needs to come holla at you himself before I make you mine, girl, you too pretty." "Anyway honey, you tripping. How you gone sell me on your man and throw a line in for yourself?" "I don't know but he better get right before I change my mind and take you for myself." "You so stupid bye boy." He rode off saying, "I'm gonna tell him to come talk to you." That's just like a negro, trying to fix me up with his buddy and his own self too.

Man I love my hood. I don't care how hot it is. They don't have any air conditioning so I know my sister has pulled the blower from the heater out and plugged up 2 or 3 fans to cool the house. That's the best we could do in all those bricks. I'm so glad I moved to Boulevard. It's the hood too but at least I have central heating and air, oh yeah and carpet. I like my place. My neighbors are incredible, and the area is pretty quiet. It's very clean and there are trees and grass. I've never lived in New York, but from all the videos and movies I've seen, I can say that this part of Boulevard looks like what New York does to me. My building has 4 units, 2 apartments at the bottom and 2 at the top. I live on the bottom. I have 2 bedrooms, so Nandi has her own space even though she still sleeps with me until I can get her a bedroom suite.

I sure do hate to go to work today, but then that's every day. What I need to do is take my dumb butt back to medical school. That's where the money is. People always need medical attention. My instructor told me if I went to school to be a physician's assistant, nine job opportunities would be available for every person who graduated at an income level of $50,000 a year and better. Damn, that sounds so good, but I'm not ready to go back to school for six years. Anyway, another dream deferred. It's time for me to get my butt up and get ready for work, and whoever this is ringing my phone off the hook is about to get cussed the hell out.

"HELLO!"
"Damn boo, did I catch you at a bad time?"
"Ooh, what's up, Rae?"
"Nothing, I thought you were probably at work."
"I can't tell. You let my phone ring 5011 times."
"Ooh shit I lost track of time watching these silly ass females on Ricky Lake argue over this fake pimp ass nigga and all he keep stressing is both of them is his hoes for life and ain't nothing gone change that."

"That's every day, and you know it."
"Skye they first cousins girl."
"More power to them. If they like it, I love it."
"See ain't nobody ask you to sum shit up. You kill me with yo white ass."

"Bitch I'm the color of brown sugar ain't nothing white about me."

"Nawl bitch not your color, your attitude.

Always trying to be providicly correct."

"What the fuck is providicly? Are you trying to say politically correct?" "You know what I'm talking about bitch? I got tongue-tied."

"Is that right? "
"Yeah."
"Shut your dumb ass up, girl. You say anything you think sounds right." "Like I said, white ass."

"Don't hate ho."
"Bitch get a grip."
"Bitch get a job."
"Oh, so you gone go there? You know I been looking for a job

and you suppose to be hooking me up with your people."

"Well, I ain't heard nothing from Norm or Eli. Anyway, your ass might get me fired with all that stealing and shit. Kleptomaniac! Bitch, you steal eyeliners, nail polish, lip gloss, and anything else you can get your sticky little hands on. All this you take from your folks, so ain't no telling what you might steal from them."

"Ohhh Skye you wrong for that."
"It's the truth and you know it!"
"Not no more."
"Bye Rae,"
"but Skye….." Too late, girl, I already hung up on your ass! Let me get ready to go.

RINGGG, RINGGG.
"What Rae?"
"You good girl, how'd you know it was me?"
"How could I not know it was your annoying ass?"
"Anyway ho."
"Your momma."
"For real you know that nigga keep asking about you."
"Who? "
"Who hell! Raheem!"

SURPRISE SURPRISE

"Ooh."
"Ooh? Bitch you need to get with him. He just hit the number for $65,000, and you know he hit three months ago for… "

"I know, I know, $13,000. That's his money. "
"Yeah, but he ain't got no problem breaking bread with you."
"Well, if it's all that's, why don't you holler at him?"
"Because he likes you."
"Yeah, whatever, Rae."
"Let me hold $20 Skye?"
"Since you are on his team and he has so much money, tell him to pay you for being the town crier, and you'll have some money."

"What the fuck is a town crier Skye?"

"Look it up in the dictionary, dumb ass I got to go get ready for work. We'll talk about all this nonsense later.

"Okay." "Don't forget to pick me up at 10:30 pm on the dot bye." I really gotta stop cussing so much. Every time I'm on the phone with that girl my mouth turns into a dumpster. Anyway, I ain't trying to feel no nigga right now. At 2 years old, Nandi takes up all my time. She my nigga for life.

Some days, I miss Zaye so much. I wish he didn't have to go back to New York. I suppose it was for the best though. He needed to get back on track because he'd been messing up in school. I think we had a really cool relationship because, for the first time in a long time, I felt like someone really cared for me, and It was the simple things that he did that made me happy, along with the fact that he knew how to touch the right spots that I'd forgotten I had. I know there's no use in hoping that he'll get it together and come back so I'll just remember the times we shared together and move on, eventually. I can say I'm not sad that he's gone because I totally understand why he had to go.

It wasn't a breakup because we weren't getting along, but his college education was starting to take a back seat to everything else. His father was adamant about him doing what he needed to do in school, and that meant going back home to New York. We talk all the time on the phone, and I guess it's just wishful thinking, but I want him to come back so that this void that I have for someone to be with will be filled.

"Skye, these flowers just came for you. I don't know who you've done it to now, but whoever it is must really like you because these cost a pretty penny." "Stop playing Norm. I don't know nothing about no flowers and I know they not for me 'cause I don't know anybody who would send me flowers unless….. Zaye sent them."

"Nawl these ain't from no Zaye, these say…."

"These say stay out of my business Norm! Big-headed butt! Who told you to read the card anyway?" (The card reads…)

You look like a lady who can appreciate nice things. These flowers will hopefully brighten your day and open up the door to a pleasant conversation tonight over dinner if you'll have me. I'm not big on poems or anything but I want you to know I think you are the most beautiful woman I know and these flowers were as close as I could come to even comparing anything to you and I had to let you know how I envision you. You're pretty as a flower. Please let me take you out to dinner. RAHEEM.

"Who is Raheem?"

"Nobody. I don't know who told him where I work at anyway. Probably dumb ass Rae. She makes me so sick always trying to fix somebody up."

"Skye, who is Raheem?"

"This dude who thinks he likes me. He's always sending messages by his flunkies that he likes me."

"What's wrong with a man liking you? I was starting to get worried that you were going to get cobwebs. You know, you not getting any and all. It's been 4 months since Zaye left, and you haven't gone out with anyone I know. Asking for all this overtime."

"There's nothing wrong with a man liking you as long as he has the balls to say something to you himself instead of having everybody else up in your business. As far as cobwebs are concerned, I'm aight. I keep some AA batteries, just call me Miss Magnesium lol. Stop worrying so much about how long it's been. I get a whole lot of action with dudes."

"Like who?"

"Meikeh, Omar, Morris, Pac, and tonight, Denzel."

"There you go with your Block Buster buddies. If you get pregnant by any of those fellows you'll have a little Soul Food with some Love and Basketball, add some Boys In the Hood a handful of Poetic Justice, then sprinkle it with a pinch of Training Day and you got a bona fide silver screen baby!"

"Hah, hah Norm you think you so funny. I just don't think I'm ready for nothing serious."

"It doesn't have to be serious. Just go out and have some fun every now and again. You act like an old woman."

"If this guy likes me, why can't he just come to me like a gentleman and tell me?"

"Maybe he's shy."
"Yeah right."
"Maybe he thinks the messages might make you curious."
"Not hardly, maybe he's a psycho." (Out of nowhere we hear.)
"Or maybe he's just taken by your beauty and doesn't think he has a chance in hell to get to know someone as wonderful as you. Maybe whenever I try to speak to you words just don't come out as easily as I would like and I don't want to make a big fool out of myself. You know *you never can get a second chance to make a first impression."*

"I'm not big on impressions. I'd prefer someone genuine."

"I assume this here is Raheem."

"In the flesh, and Skye, this is for you because since the moment I first saw you when I was in the 2nd grade, you had my heart. So please accept this heart pendant necklace as a token of our hopeful friendship."

"Skye, can I talk to you for a minute?"
"Sure… Excuse me for a second, Raheem.
What's up Norm?"
Did this boy just creep up in here while we were talking and start a whole conversation?….
Did I just hear him say since he was in the second grade?"
"Yep."
"How long have you known him?"
"Apparently since elementary school, but at the present I don't remember him though."

"He's been stalking you! Ever since elementary school!"

"Stop being silly. That boy don't really remember me, he just knows that we went to the same school."

"Anyway, watch him. He looks funny, big head with a mole right in the center; something ain't right. He looks like he thinks too much about nothing. I hate to hurt him for trying to fuck over you. Coming in here with his flowers and jewelry."

"Well, look at you—all protective and stuff. First, you want me to go out and have fun, stop acting like an old woman, and get rid of my cobwebs. Now I need to watch him. He's harmless. Anyway, I like flowers, and I love jewelry!"

"Yeah, but nothing in life is free."
"So I shouldn't accept it, huh?"
"Hell yeah you gone take it."
"Norm, you're confusing me to death lol."
"He might be a good kid Skye, just watch him."
"I promise I won't get into anything I don't want to be apart of."
"Sometimes we get caught up and It ain't as easy to get out of situations as it is to get into them. Sometimes a love won't let go."

"Okay daddy."

"You damn right I'm your daddy! Or the next best thing to him. I'll kill a rock over you."

"You so sweet Norm, I'll be fine. Besides, I haven't even told him I'll go out with him yet. Let's just see how that goes first."

"I sure wish Zaye hadn't left. Now that was a good kid. I liked you with him."

"I miss him to Norm, but the facts remain the same. He's gone and he's not coming back and neither one of us can afford a long distance relationship. So we both have to move on, well you that is because Zaye and I already have. Now let me get back out front because I've been gone 10 minutes too long."

"So what's up Skye?"

"Ooh, I didn't mean to be gone that long I had to clear some things up with my boss."

"I wasn't rushing you. I would wait a lifetime for you. I already have."

"Listen you ain't got to lie to kick it."

"I'm not lying. If you give me a chance I'll show you I can make you the happiest woman alive. "

"Look Raheem, you really don't have to pour it on so thick. I mean I like the flowers, but the necklace was totally unexpected. You don't even know me that well, and you're buying me gifts like that."

"Skye I'm straight. If I couldn't afford it I wouldn't have bought it."

"The question isn't if you can afford it or not but what do you expect for it?"

"I don't expect anything. I was in the mall and I saw it and thought about you like I do all the time."

"Spare me the niceties ok Raheem. What's up?"

"Skye I'm the right man and I'm just looking for the right woman and I feel like you're the one I want to invest my time and energy in. Just give me the chance to show you. Pleasssse!"

"Ok I'll go out with you but my baby has to come too. I hardly do anything without her, we're a package deal. If she can't go then I can't go."

"Oh nah Skye I would never exclude your daughter…Raheem loves the kids. I have a little girl too. So what time can I come pick ya'll up?"

"I didn't say tonight Raheem, I am still at work and when I get off tonight I'm going to get my baby and go home. So let's start off by exchanging numbers then we'll take it from there, sir." "Ok I can go for that."

(…a few months later) "Skye, Zaye just got here wit some dude. He says he didn't want to just pop up unannounced but he didn't have a way to contact you. He says he just wants to get his stuff but you know I don't have a key to your closet where a lot of his stuff is. Can you come home so he can get his stuff?"

"Tell him I'll be there in about 20 minutes." "Aight, can you bring me some Mikey D's on your way?"

"Can you pay me when I get there?"

"I don't have any money." "So that means you gonna be hungry huh?" "Man pleasssse??"

"I got you, but I want my money when you get paid."

"Raheem, I need to go home so I can let Zaye in to get his stuff." "Why Teaon can't let him in to get his stuff."
"Because Teaon doesn't have a key to my closet and that's my house and I don't want nobody snooping around my stuff when I'm not there."
"Why you think he gonna snoop around?"
"I don't think he will, I'm just not sure. You know how people do when you not around, looking in your drawers, going through your mail, you know just being nosey."

"Naw you might just be trying to get with that nigga."
"Puhlease! I'm good. I got what I want. Besides, Zaye knows that I'm with you and he ain't coming at me like that. Anyway

why don't you come with me if you think that its like that."
"Naw I trust you. Just call me when you finish and we'll hook up later." "Alright baby I call you in a little bit."

Oh my God, I can't believe that Zaye is really here. I really miss not talking to him the past few months, but I had to cut all ties to make sure that what I'm trying to develop with Raheem is right. That ain't stop me from thinking about him from time to time. I wonder what he's looking like. Knowing Zaye the way I do be looking good. He's always on that fly New York shit. Check out my boo trying to get jealous. He should've come with me if he was that insecure. Even though he has no reason to be. I'm really starting to dig him. As soon as I pull up to my apartment I see this jet black Navigator and I know Zaye is driving this whip. I am so nervous about seeing him I don't know how I'm gonna react. God please let Zaye look like the last junkie so I won't be tempted. I really want to do this the right way. Lips on glossy? Check. Hair on point? Check. Bvlgari on deck? Check. Am I putting a hurting on this Mecca outfit or what? Please believe it! So I'm looking good, smelling good and my stomach has knots in it. Why if I'm not checking for Zaye? I don't know but I know I want him to loose his mind when he sees me and how good I look. I walked in the door and I find this dude that I don't know blowing smoke in the air. No doubt it's that shit but I don't know this dude from Adams cat so umma have to check his ass.

"Bruh, who are you and why you got my place looking like I just set off a roach bomb?"
"My bad miss lady, Zgod said it was cool, didn't mean no disrespect ma. My name Bron, um his cousin."
"Who the hell is Zgod? You mean Zaye?"
"Yeah that's what at said Zaye."

"No you said Zgod."
"Yeah same thing alike."
"Whatever bruh, you high. Where this negro at so I can check

his ass for making you think it was cool for you to feel at home."
"Damn miss lady my bad. He in the back room packing some stuff up."
"Sweetie the name is Skye."
"It got to be, it wouldn't fit nobody but you. Again, no disrespect to you ma, you pretty as hell and feisty. I don't know how that man left you and came back to the NY. It had to be by force 'cause a man don't just get up and choose to leave his earth, that'll kill him. I see why bruh been looking like he just sitting by the dock of the bay watching that mufucka dry all the way up just wasting time."

I had to smile a little on that one. That's a NY negro for you always trying to sound profound like they kicking some deep shit when they saying something to you. Which, I happen to like. At least they switch it up and don't use the same lame ass line, (baby you look so good I'll drank your bath water)

…….. I enter the back room "Ahh excuse me, who is dude in the living room getting his smoke on?"
"That's the first thing you say to me and you haven't seen me in months? Take me to see Nandi."
"Um just saying Zaye."
"Skye come on she right round the corner and I don't know when I'll get a chance to see her again."
"Aight."
"That's my poo-poo."
"She's at school having P.E. now it's 11:45."
"Okay let's do this and I'll explain who puff the magic dragon is when we get back."
"So we just gone leave him here while we go out?"
"Sky that's my mans and you know I would never put you in harms way. That man got your back just like me and besides he good people."

"Okay."
"Aight we on the same page now?"

"Yeah."
" One!"
"Mommy!"

"Hey punkin."

"Nay Nay!"

"Hey Zaye!.... Zaye cameeee back, Zaye cameeee back."

"I came back just to see you kiddo."

"You gone stay with us again?"

" Not right now baby girl but um gonna be in touch with you all the time okay?"

"What did you bring me?"

"Punkin you not suppose to ask people for stuff."

"People? Since when did I become people? She can ask me for what ever, you on the other hand bet not ask me for nada lol!"

"You are such an asshole Zaye."

"I'm just joking, when I'm being serious."

"Oh you got jokes?"

"Nah for real baby girl I'm gonna leave it with your mom so when you get out of school she can take you to buy whatever you want okay?"

"Okay Zaye. I miss you."

"Word? That's what's up. I miss you and your mommy too much. Can I have a hug? (mauh) Thank you, thank you, thank you sweetie I'll see you next time."

"Bye bye Zaye."

"Bye kiddo."

"Ok baby, mommy will be back to get you when school is out."

"Ok mommy....don't be late like you was last time cause I'm

gonna be the only one left and I don't want to be the only one left cause then umma cry."

" I promise I won't be late. I'm glad you had the chance to see her."

"Me too. That's my baby. Hey before I forget, this is just a little something for whatever you need it for."

"I'm good Zaye you don't have to do this."

"Skye let me be a man. You held me down and you didn't have too. A few ends ain't nothing compared to the love you showed me and my family. I love you girl and I always will. Now take this money and let's get back to the crib before Bron steals your sofa or something."

" Shut up Zaye."

When we got back to the house all I could think about was how I knew this man loved my daughter and how I knew my daughter loved this man. We get back to the house and I'm making a mad dash to the bathroom! "Move Zaye um in a tight, I have to use the bathroom."

When I came out of the bathroom I was greeted with "Heyyy Caramel Sundae."

My Goodness, please don't let him start. That was my nick name he gave me. Caramel Sundae. He got his arms open looking at me and licking his lips like I was the last time he tasted blackberry molasses. So I got to give him a hug right? It's just common courtesy? As I walked into an embrace that felt like it was formatted just for me, I felt what it must feel like to find something you thought you had lost forever. It was firm like he could've squeezed all the air out of my lungs, yet gentle enough to make me want to never breathe again.

He smelled so damn good, like rain. Earthy, woodsy, sweaty, manly. He smelled like Joop cologne mixed with the aroma of a Philly Blunt. The same Philly Blunt that was being smoked by his cousin Bron in my living room. I heard a faint sound, almost a far away cry calling "Zayeeeee" and I knew my yoni was about to make her presence known.

As I attempted to let go and regain my composure he held on a little longer secured my hands behind my back and whispered in my ear how much he missed me and wanted me. All at the same time trailing warm syrupy sweet kisses down my neck. I was mush. My knees were trembling and my yoni was like liquid fire with a heartbeat. Thumping! - It felt like I had a bad toothache in between my legs. I wanted to grab my yoni and just hold her, cover her mouth to muffle her cries of needing to be touched and sucked the way she remembered. But I couldn't grab her for fear that I just might scorch my fingers. And I didn't want Zaye to know that I needed him even if only for that brief moment. It's like he heard my thoughts or something cause he pulled his lips from my neck and said, "you say something?" "I said no."

DID I DO THAT

I then realized he had heard something alright, and it wasn't me moaning softly. It was my yoni screaming at him to do what he did best. She just wouldn't shut the fuck up. As soon as I felt his breath on my neck I knew I wanted him all up inside of me. I didn't want to fuck him, I just wanted him to touch me with those phenomenal hands and lick my nipples until I had cum. He must've known because he led me inside my bedroom and closed the door. He laid me across the bed and began to unbutton my shirt. I didn't protest even though I probably should've. I had told another man that I was his and I had no intentions on cheating on him but I was so hot and so wet. So horny; not to mention that I hadn't had an orgasm with Raheem once since we had been together.

Zaye just knew me so well and I figured that if I just let him suck on my nipples that I could have that release I craved so badly. That was the awesome thing about Zaye. He could make me have orgasms just by licking and sucking on my nipples. Plus he had the Midas touch. I loved the way he touched my yoni, and I would cum like that too. He started to nibble at my bra while rubbing my yoni through my pants. I wanted to tell him to stop but I couldn't. At that very moment any remaining thoughts of Raheem disappeared and I only wanted the release that came from a man who took his time to please you. I was so grateful I didn't have to pleasure myself to get what I longed for. He unhooked my bra from in front with his teeth and slowly pulled my left nipple into his mouth and sighed like he had been waiting on this day forever. As he fondled with my right-breast I started to feel like my yoni was gnawing at my pants trying to claw her way free. I stopped him long enough to pull my pants down. He was teasing me sucking and licking, flicking his tongue back and forth over each nipple, making me squirm and moan "baby please touch it." But he wouldn't. He kept me at bay by sticking his tongue into my mouth and back to my nipples again. Then he asked, "do you want me to put my finger right there?" And pointed at my yoni. I said "yes; desperately." He told me to say please and I replied "baby please touch her don't you see she making a mess? Slobbing everywhere, got my legs all sticky. She screaming for you, can't you make her stop? She misses you so fucking much. Please Zaye make me cum like you use too."

My lingo had no limits when it came to my libido.–It ain't no telling what I might say. What ever comes up comes out. I'm not shy at all when it comes to sexually expressing myself. "How can I say no when you put it like that?" He started to draw small slow deliberate circles around my clit with his finger. I immediately started to release the beginnings of a pre orgasm. As he was licking my nipple he said, "If you get greedy and cum, I'm gonna stop." I knew I was going to loose my mind if he stopped. So I held back, suppressing that feeling of wanting and needing to release. He told me he wanted to play a game, see how long I could take the pain and the pleasure of holding my climax at bay. He told me to say the alphabet backwards. "WWhat? How? What do you mean? I mean, I can't concentrate!" How in the hell did he expect me to say the fucking alphabet backwards when I'm so disheveled right now that I couldn't say it the way it's supposed to be said. "You are so sadistic!"

"True, but you like it." I cannot tell a lie, I did. So I start saying the damn alphabet backwards and fucked it all up. "Z, Y, X, W, V, T."
"Start over Skye you messed up."
"Z, Y, X, W, V, V, V, U, T, S, oooh baby don't stop." "You better stop talking and keep reciting."
"Baby I can't do this."
"Yes you can, I have faith in you, start over."
"Damn it Zaye it feels like my yoni is going to explode!"

He was swirling his finger around my clit, then he'd dip it into my yoni until his hand was at the base of my mound and his finger could go no further. Then he started to rub my g-spot which drove me insane. I could feel sweat starting to form at the base of my neck. My feet felt like they were burning and my nipples were as hard as chocolate chips. So I licked my fingers to moisten them and started to rub them back and forth squeezing them wishing I could suck them myself. He stopped rubbing and started fingering me slowly with his right finger then he pushed back the hood covering my ~~clit~~ and pressed down on it with his left thumb. Making me gasp for air and curse everybody on the planet "fuck, fuck, fuckkk!!"

Then he stopped and said, "I'm waiting."
"Waiting for what?"
"Waiting for you ~~to~~ keep going."
"Okay, okay Zaye just don't stop again Z, Y, X, fuuuuuck, babyyyyy!! W, V, U, T, T, T, S, S, S, baby Zaye , Oh my God it feels, R, Q, P, P, please don't stop."

His fingers were slipping in and out of me rubbing and squeezing and he was licking my nipples my God I didn't know if this was real! He asked me if I liked it, if I missed it, if I wanted to cum all over his fingers. I said "Like water for chocolate."

He said he missed me so much. That I smelled so good like peaches and vanilla ice cream. He said my skin was so soft and smooth like butter. I asked him if I could cum now and he slowed down and said," Skye man I missed you sooo much. That nigga treating you right?"

"I mumbled yeah."

"He making this pussy wet up like this?"

I shook my head no.

"I know damn well he ain't. Um the only man know how to make my pussy scream. I heard her calling me when I started kissing your neck. She communicates with me you my sexpot."

I smiled. Then he put my nipple back in his mouth and started slurping it and it drove me crazy.

"You wanna cum Skye?"

"Yesss."

"Lift your left leg up and hold it. I know how you get when you cum so I promise to stroke it lightly so you won't kill yourself."

I wanted to fall off this cliff I was on and die the way he's making me feel right now. So he sucking my nipple, massaging my clit, dipping his finger deep down inside my yoni and um hunching on his fingers begging him not to stop and this negro slows down and puts pressure on my clit and asks me if I love him. And I said,"Like a fat kid loves cake." He smiled.

I asked him why he keeps playing with me torturing me like this.

"I want you to remember us like this for the rest of your life. Who knows when we will see each other again?"

"Okay baby" was all I could say. Then he brought me back to nirvana and I felt like I was loosing consciousness. I was dizzy and lightheaded. Every part of my body tingled and felt like I had been electrocuted.

He said, "Now you can cum for me Skye." He kissed me with the passion of a newly engaged couple. I arched my back as he simultaneously pinched my nipple and rubbed my clit faster. My yoni started having spasms and my ears started ringing I spoke into his mouth while he kissed me, "Oh shit, right there bay, bay baby, phuckkk, get it daddy, daddy, mmnhh, mmnh, ohhhh daddy um cumming, um cumming, um cumming!!!!!!!!!!!"

As he stroked me to ecstasy he slowed down but didn't stop. Just barley touched me, sucked and licked my nipple as I started my descent from pure unadulterated bliss. I loved when he did that because my clit is so sensitive after an orgasm of that magnitude, to keep rubbing as vigorously would only make it unbearable and it doesn't allow me to fully ride the wave all the way out. Stroking it slightly permitted me to understand that he was genuinely into pleasing me and making me lose my mind. Which only made me cum again and one more time before I had to beg him to stop. My legs were shaking so bad.

He held me and kissed me with such tenderness. "Skye if you cumming like that I know that niggga ain't fucking you right. You got a puddle in the bed that look like a small pond." "Zaye why you got to go there right after what we just experienced? Don't ruin it for me okay?" "Um just saying babey I wanted to eat that yoni but I know you and dude doing your thing so I ain't want to go there no what I mean ma? But from the looks of things bruh ain't doing nothing!" "You want to hit this don't you?" " Nah my love, I did what I wanted to do. Just knowing that I alone possess the power to make you bust like that, is satisfaction enough. Whenever you want it done right Skye we can arrange a trip to the NY just for you baby." How unselfish was he? Nobody else but a New York nigga do you that. I got up after a few minutes so I could get myself together. I felt so calm and at peace. I was smiling from the inside out. I didn't know how much I needed that release. I just felt really good.

Once we were straight he asked me if I would ride with him to pick up something his dad had asked him to get while he was in the A. I said cool and me, him and Bron dipped. We talked about old times with Bron and how we first met at Club 112. Stopped by Busy Bee's restaurant and grubbed on turkey wings macaroni and cheese, turnip greens, corn bread and some bomb ass sweet tea. On the way back home Zaye asked me if I was happy. I said, "Um good." Um talking about with ole dude? I said, "He's cool. We have fun. I mean he really likes me and I'm learning to like him too. He's good to me Zaye."

"How does he treat Nandi?" "He's good with her. I just know that this has been a hard transition for me because I still think about you a lot and I know we didn't break up because our shit was messed up but because you had to go home or go to jail. Our thing was so real. Now it's like starting over trying to fill a void with someone who is trying to show you love."

"That's what's up shorty. I would never tell you to hold it

down for me and stop the movement. Truth be told I don't know when I'll see the A again. NY is my home probably for a couple of years, until get back on track. I want you to be happy. You deserve it. You're a good girl. This nigga lucky as hell and don't know it."

When we got back to the crib Teon says, "Raheem called you and I told him you went out the door."

"Oh okay I'll call him in a minute. We went to see Nandi and she was so happy to see Zaye. Teon get out the bathroom girl I got to pee."

Zaye said, "I gotta pee too."

"Well I'm first."

I came out after I finished and Zaye went in. I was heading to my bedroom to start getting his hats off the wall when I heard knock, knock knock.

"Teon get the door please."

"I can't I got this perm on my hands."

"Aight big face, I got it." I opened the door and Raheem kinda startled me. I wasn't expecting to see him. Zaye-was just coming out of the bathroom with his tank top on and his t-shirt thrown across his shoulder.

"What's up bruh?" Raheem look at me like Zaye hadn't just spoke to him and asked me where I been. I said, "We went to see Nandi" and he punched me in my face. My nose started bleeding and my first instinct was to run and I did. I ran over to another apartment building and stood in the stairwell. I was so scared and embarrassed. I didn't know if he and Zaye were going at it or what. After about 30 minutes, I finally went back home still scared.

When I got in the house Teon asked me if I was alright. I just went into the bathroom and tried to clean my face up. A few minutes later I heard voices in the living room. I came out of the bathroom and it was Raheem. I just looked at him.

"Give me my got damn necklace." I was nervous and I didn't want him to hit me again so I walked toward the bedroom and he followed behind me. I was almost trembling and I started to fumble with the clasp on the necklace around my neck.

"Why the fuck didn't you answer the phone?"

"I wasn't here. Teon told me you called when I got back from the day care center."

"What the fuck you doing over there?"

"I took Zaye to see Nandi."

"Why?"

"Cause he asked me to take him to see her."

"So you just took her out of school so he could see her?"

"No. Zaye is still on the list to pick her up. I never thought to take him off. Anyway we didn't go inside. They were outside at recess and we went to the fence and talked with her."

"Bitch I been sitting outside waiting on you for a long time. Hurry up and give me my shit. I should've known not to fuck with you. You ain't shit."

I gave him the necklace, he picked my purse up off the dresser took the car keys out and swung at my face with my bag. I tried to shield my face with my hand and the bag hit it hard, breaking my left forefinger. It looked a crooked mess. I stood there in shock and said, "You broke my finger!"

He didn't say anything. Just turned around and walked out. I left out the door after I knew he was gone and used my girl Pooh's car to go to Georgia Baptist Hospital, which was two minutes from where I lived in 4th ward on Boulevard.

As I sat in the doctor's office looking at my deformed finger, I just couldn't believe that he put his hands on me. I never had a clue that this was who he was. No one ever mentioned in their haste to set us up that he was known to fight women. The doctor came in and told me that from the x-ray I had chipped bone fragments in my finger and that he was going to inject the finger with a numbing medicine so he could reset it and that I would have to wear a cast from my finger to my elbow to ensure that it would be stable and could start to mend. I would also have to start ~~taking~~ therapy to learn how to use the finger again. I was humiliated.

"Ms, I don't know how or why this happened to you. I suspect this is a case of domestic violence. You can report this to the police and they will arrest the person who did this to you. You are really a beautiful young lady and if this person put his hands on you once then this is only the beginning of the worst nightmare you can imagine. It will never get better, only worse." I just looked at him and felt sorry for myself. I told him thank you for the information and I would think about what he said. I took my prescription and left.

As I drove to the drugstore I thought how much worse it could've been. Had he come an hour or so earlier I would've been caught dead to the wrong, enjoying the treatment that Zaye was giving me. But he hadn't come earlier so he didn't catch anything. I was wrong. I allowed another man to touch what Raheem deemed as his. Maybe he sensed that something went on but like I said he didn't catch anything so in my eyes he was more wrong than I was. He put his hands on me because he called me and I wasn't in the house to answer his call. When he saw Zaye coming out of the bathroom all kind of thoughts filled his head. He still could've asked me without putting his hand on me. He punched me in the face like I was a man. He broke my finger. He scared me and embarrassed me. Lord knows how my mom is going to react when she hears about it, she don't play that shit. She has been known to shoot at and stab a negro. And how am I suppose to tell Nandi what happened to mommy's hand? I don't ever want to see him again.

I woke up this morning with a throbbing headache. I don't know where it came from. Oh yeah……; I almost got knocked the fuck out yesterday! My finger is feeling like it's about to explode. I guess I'll take one of the 800 Motrin prescribed by my doctor so I can think clearly about what's my next move. As I look down at my cast, I still can't believe he did this to me. We've only been together for 3 months and he put his hands on me in anger. Now I'm going to have to explain this to all my girls, my family and Lord forbid my boss Norm.

"So what happened to your hand lil girl?" Norm asked.

"Nothing. Playing around with Raheem, Nandi and I fell and I twisted my wrist."

" Dang what kind of playing were yall doing?"

"I don't even know it all happened so fast. One minute we were wrestling around and the next I was pent down with my arm behind my back and there you go my finger was broke."

"That sounds kind of bazaar, but I guess stuff like that can happen when you're horse playing. You just better be glad nothing happened to that baby while you were out there acting a fool."

I don't know how much longer I can keep this lying up. It seems the more I try to hide what happened from Norm his investigative self finds a way to turn my story upside down. The sad thing is that he's right. I'm just too embarrassed to tell him the truth. I feel so stupid and on top of that I've been talking to Raheem. I mean he has apologized over and over again. I guess he's really sorry. He was just so upset with the thought of me being with someone else and he overreacted that's all. I know one thing, if he tries something like that again um not messing with him no more.

It's been almost 3 weeks and things seem pretty much back to the way they were. As I dropped Nandi off to school she told me to be careful and don't break my finger again. I smiled at her and I told her I promise I wouldn't. As I drove off I started to feel some kind of way about what happened that day he put his hands on me. It didn't make matters any better that my mom called and said she would be over in a while and she wanted to talk to me. I was so not looking forward to whatever she wanted to talk about. I have to go to the grocery store and then get home so I can cook and have dinner ready when Nandi gets home from daycare. Lord ain't no telling what she want to talk about. It's not that often she comes over. Must be important.

Boy I swear whoever it is knocking like the police finna get it."

WHO IS IT!!!!!?" I yelled as I opened the door. My momma and her ole man Lucky were standing there looking like a geriatric version of Foxy Brown and Shaft. She had on some tight blue jean bell bottoms, a yellow halter top and a grey pocketbook with white tassels hanging from it that was way too big for a woman her size to be carrying. She was only 4' 7 and 110lbs soaking wet. However; she was a force to be reckoned with. She did not play the radio, period. We all knew not to mess with Ms. Lil Bit. That's what everybody called her. Ms. Lil Bit. Even though she was a small lady she was known to slang a mean blade and didn't mind shooting her pearl handle 45 if need be.

Lucky had on a beige safari pantsuit with a purple, yellow, and green scarf tied around his neck. He had on dark shades and about seven rings on both hands. He smelled like Old Spice and baby powder. He reminded me of Thurston Howell III from Gilligan's Island, the way he dressed. He talked with conviction, like everything he said was matter of fact. He had a presence about him that made you want to believe everything he said was truth. It was said he had some underground connections with men's whose names you didn't speak on but you knew could take care of things and make problems or should I say people disappear, if you know what I mean. Now I don't know if it's true or not. I'm just telling you things I've heard. He was a smooth joker. I almost laughed at the way the twosome looked but the expression on my mom's face let me know that she wasn't in a laughing mood.

"Hey ma, come on in." I hugged her as she entered. "Hey dad I kissed his cheek when he entered." In my attempt to make small conversations I said, It's hot outside toda,y ain't it? Yall want some iced tea or something to drink?" Lucky said tea was fine with him. Momma didn't say she wanted anything. So I fixed both of them some ice tea and asked them what wind blew them to my side of town? Lucky said, "Your mom wanted to talk to you about some stuff that was on her mind but I'll let her tell you."

"You ain't got to speak for me Lucky, I know how to damn talk."

" Ma….. why you so hostile?"

MY MOMMA DON'T PLAY

"Why did you lie to me?"

"About what?"

"Don't play dumb with me Skye! What happened to your finger?"

"I already told you I was at work trying to move some boxes and……."

"Move some boxes my ass. That niggaa broke your finger and um gon break his ass now watch me. Where the bastard at?"

She started walking through the apartment like she was hoping to find him here. She came back to the living room and said "you may as well tell me where his punk ass at and pick your mouth up off the floor while you at it."

"Ma I didn't want to tell you cause I knew you was going to react like you're doing now."

"What in the hell do you mean I was going to react like I am now. How in the hell do you expect me to react? You're my child. I went through 11 ½ hours of labor bringing you into this world. I'm the one that stayed down at that hospital with you when you got shot everyday all day. I'm the one got your back and you can depend on when you can't depend on nobody else. I know you. I know when you hurt, when you happy and when you hiding something. I raised you and I pray to God I ain't raised no fool!"

"Your heart is too big and too open. You're always trying to please somebody. You're looking for love in all the wrong places. You don't have to look for it baby. When it's time God will send him to you.

You are a beautiful special young lady and he don't deserve you. I love you and I wouldn't tell you nothing wrong. Now I know I don't live here but I want his ass out of here today! He can't sleep here another night and I meant that! Tell him I said so. I gotta go right now before I lose my religion, but I will be back to check and see if his ass still living here and I won't be by myself. I swear fo God if I catch him anywhere um gon buss a cap in his ass! Walking round here like he run something. He don't run shit but his mouth. Booger wolf looking son of a bitch!"

"Calm down Lil Bit."

"Don't tell me to calm down! That motherfucker put his hands on my baby. Broke her fucking finger! I will kill that bastard! Don't tell me to calm down Lucky, that's my child!"

She started walking out the door and she was crying, but she was still talking big shit….."motherfucker gon put his hands on my baby! He must don't know who he fucking with. He rather walk through hell with gasoline draws on than to fuck with me! He rather fuck with Qaddafi than to fuck with me!"

Lucky got up and followed behind her. He didn't say a word, not because he was scared to but because he had her back 100%. He turned to me just as he was walking out the door and said, "Leave that boy alone, this is just the beginning of some shit you can spare yourself and your mamma."

Then he walked away. As I closed the door the warm air that rushed in seemed to have made my mouth dry and I almost struggled to swallow the lump that had formed in my throat. It wasn't until then that I realize my mouth was still hanging open. My mamma was no joke. I wonder who told her what really happened. She making me put my man out of my house. Who did she think she was? I'm a grown woman. I can handle my own business.

Yeah right, who am I kidding? She did say she would be back and I know she'll make good on her word. And if she sees him anywhere, she is gon shoot at him. If she'll shoot at her own kids, I know she won't spare him.

I arrived at my doctor's office today at 1:00pm for my first physical therapy appointment. The physical therapist is a white girl in her late 20's. She's wearing jeans, sneakers and a grey t-shirt that read "this is going to be a challenge but you can do it." The clinic has all kinds of equipment for physical rehabilitation. There are whirlpools, massage tables, weights of various sizes and several stretching pulleys.

"Hello Ms. Patterson my name is Elaine and I'm going to be your therapist for today. After reviewing your chart I see that you have a digitus secundus manus injury resulting from some sort of physical trauma that you've suffered. Am I right?"

She was looking like I should know what she was talking about, and I did because I was a certified medical assistant which ain't no doctor but I knew a lil sumn sumn. I simply replied that the middle phalanx was pushed up over the proximal phalanx which caused bone fragments to chip. I then said we could keep throwing around fancy medical terminology that the average person wouldn't know or we could just talk like regular people since I am going to be your patient for a while and I want to feel comfortable talking to you. Shoot, yeen gotta impress me I recognized your credentials.

She smiled and said, "You're right, I'm just so use to going with patient etiquette that it never occurred to me to slow down and just talk. I apologize, I never wanted to make you feel uncomfortable. So with that being said let's get started."

I smiled.

"We're going to start off by placing a holder around your finger sort of like a small rubber band. Then we will emerge your hand in a really warm solution called paraffin wax for about five minutes. This will allow the ligaments in your finger to soften and relax so that when we remove the finger band you will have more flexibility in the tendons in your finger. Any questions?"

"Is it going to hurt?"

"It may be a little painful but once you've finished all your sessions, which will be about 12 you will have regained at least 90 percent of usage in your finger. Sounds good?"

She seems so happy go lucky. I wonder what her life is like. I wonder if she's ever been in an abusive relationship. Probably not. She probably grew up in Buckhead in one of those big fancy houses with a father that spoiled her with everything she wanted. Definitely went to private school and vacationed in the Pocono's. Trying to sound cool I said, "Yeah I need my finger."

"Ms. Patterson,"……

"You can call me Skye if you want."

"Okay, Skye.

"Listen I don't know your story but I have witnessed enough domestic violence in my life to recognize some of the signs of a person who is being abused. My mom died at the hands of a very abusive boyfriend when I was 13. She always made excuses for the bruises on her body. She would never talk to me or anybody about what she was going through. She believed that she deserved the treatment he gave her because she provoked him. She felt she should just learn to keep her mouth closed so he wouldn't be mad. She stayed with him for 2 years. One day we were playing dress up and I combed her hair and put her on makeup and she put me on makeup. We were having so much fun! He came in the house with a bottle of beer, cursing loud and mad about something. He looked at her, not us and asked her where she thought she was going? She said nowhere. He said she was trying to be slick and he just caught her before she went out to whore with some dude. She tried to tell him that we were playing dress up and she wasn't going anywhere. He called her a lying whore and before she could explain any further he swung and hit her in the head. The bottle broke and he stabbed her 7 times in her face, neck and chest. She died right in front of me. I called 911 when he called her a whore because I knew where this was going. He sat on the sofa after he saw that she wasn't moving anymore and cried.

When the police came he was still holding the broken bottle. I was devastated. No child should have to witness their mother being killed. I mean I don't know your story and I don't know if you have kids but if you are going through anything like that then I am encouraging you to find the strength to leave it alone. Don't put your kids and family in that devastation that I felt and still feel. You may think that it's not my business, but if no one has ever told you that you are worth more than your weight in gold times ten, times ten, times ten million then it is my business."

A lone tear rolled down her cheek. I smiled weakly and said I was sorry about her mom. I thanked her for being concerned but assured her it wasn't my story, but she knew better than that. She said ok.

Before I left she gave me some pamphlets on battered women. One of the pamphlets said, Domestic violence…..it's everybody's business. I told her I would see her next week. As I started to walk down the street I thought, here I am about to judge this lady on what neighborhood she grew up in and all the fancy things she must have had growing up just assuming! I felt so guilty for my thoughts. That's usually what people do when they don't know something, we assume. This lady knew my card, called it and didn't bluff. I still kept the poker face though. She knew more about me than I wanted to admit. Had experienced domestic violence with her own eyes. Had lost her mother and still found her way. She wanted to do for me what she couldn't do for her mother…….she wanted to save me. Lord knows I didn't want that to be my story. Could Raheem really kill me? I don't want to think about this anymore. I gotta go pick Nandi up from school in 2 ½ hours and I really need to take a nap. When I got home I took an 800mg ibuprofen and fell asleep.

I dreamt I was a little girl in Thomasville giving the kids in the neighborhood flying lessons. Don't laugh. There is this sidewalk that forms a square around the playground right in back of our apartment. I would say it's about 100 or so feet long on each side. It encloses the monkey bars that I hung upside on too long and caught a nosebleed from, the swing set that hung way to low to the ground and cause me to bust open my big toe when I swung back down and didn't remember to tuck my legs. There was the merry go round that was lopped sided and rusty and the two rocking horses that had no handles so you were on your on and it made a noise that sounded worse than screeching chalk when you made them rock. The playground was big enough for us to play softball or kickball and we all risked our lives jumping on and hitting backflips on old dirty pissy mattresses. We loved it there. Anyway back to my dream you were laughing about. I could fly! I would teach the kids how to fly by giving them lessons flying around the perimeter of the playground over the sidewalks. I see the look on my face as I am flying and I look soooooo happy. I tell one of my students to watch me, hold your arms by your side like this. I start off running real fast, spread my arms straight out so that I look like a cross and I lift off the ground effortlessly. I coast around the playground two or three times like a bird, I even do a few stunts flipping and turning over. I see everybody below me looking up pointing at me saying wow look at Skye, that girl can fly her butt off, as if it's normal to see people flying everyday. The kids are amazed. Some of them get it, others don't but we keep practicing. I don't know why I still remember that dream like it was yesterday. It's not the first time I dreamt that dream. It always makes me feel good inside. When I woke up it was ten minutes after six and I was late getting Nandi from school.

Oh Lord I overslept. I hurry up and leave the house to go get my baby. When I get there she was sitting at her desk with another little girl whose mom was late picking her up too. I apologized to her teacher for being late and went straight to Nandi and told her I was sorry for being late. She just hugged my neck and said its okay momma I knew you were coming to get me. I kissed her and said you're right I will always come and get you. For a treat I took her to get ice cream. When we got back there was a card in the door that said I was in the neighborhood give me a call. I didn't recognize the name so I thought it was for Raheem. I brought it in the house and left it on the dresser. Once we got settled and I gave Nandi a bath and fed her and she watched Barney. I was cool with that because it gave me time to clean the kitchen get our clothes ironed for tomorrow and take a shower. Yeah I give big shouts out to Barney, he held me down for a couple of years. I didn't have any problems out of Nandi when Barney was on. Around eight forty five Nandi was knocked out.

Raheem got home about nine thirty and I fixed his plate, spaghetti with Italian sausage, garlic bread, corn on the cob and salad. We were watching something on tv all cuddled up and I thought about the card and said, "Oh it was a card on the door today with a number on it for you."

Raheem looked at the card and said, "I don't know who this is let me call the number." I was laying at the bottom of the bed and he was laying at the top when he made the call. I was looking at him while he was on the phone trying to figure out who the person was that left the card. He was talking and said, "Oh okay hold on." and handed me the phone. I said hello and it was a guy on the phone that said this Malikei. I said," Ohhhh hey whats up Mal.

"Hey Skye I just got back from Cali and I remembered you stayed on Boulevard. I was trying to get in touch with my girl Rakel. When the last time you talked to her?"

"I talked to her yesterday and she doing good. You want me to give her your number? She gon be surprised to hear from you. How long you been gone two or three years?"

"I wish I could tell you it won't happen again but I don't want to lie to you anymore. I'm sorry I disappointed you Norm. You were always so much more to me than a boss.

Thank you for the opportunity to work for you. I love you like a father and I'll miss you."

"I love you too Skye take care of yourself and Nandi. I will see you later."

I leave with my final check for $375.00 and I say my goodbyes to my now former coworkers feeling embarrassed because they all know that I just got let go. I go get into the car that Raheem let me drive and I started crying. Not because I had lost my job but because it felt like I had lost a friend. I'm finally in control of my emotions and I head to Thomasville to break Raheem the news.

"Hey Ms. Shaw how you doing today?"

"I'm fine baby how you doing?"

"I'm ok. I came by to meet Raheem here so we can go get something to eat."

"Ole chile that fool a be here in a minute cause he bringing Chayla over here to stay the night. Nandi can stay too if you want. They ain't gonna be doing nothing but watching Barney all night."

"Lol you right, you cant get a word out of them when Barney is on."

"I don't know how many times I had to sing (…I love you, you love me we're a happy family…….) with them girls. Shelby not coming up this weekend?"

"Nah she got an ear infection and her momma gon keep her home."

"Oh ok umma have to call Mashay and check on my lil baby. Nandi can stay. I know when she see Chayla she gonna want to stay anyway. I can't pull those two apart when they are together."

"So where you wanna go eat at?"

"I wanna try Rays On The River."

"Oh you must've been there with some other nigga?" "I said I want try it out….that means I've never been there. Why you always gotta go there?" We get to the restaurant and it is beautiful inside. Dimly lit with candles burning atop linen table cloths, lovely wall art, and a wonderful view of the Chattahoochee River. We stayed log enough to have a drink but dinner was horrible. On the way home I told him about losing my job and he didn't seem upset about it. I truly believe he wanted me to stop working there anyway so he would know where I was 24/7. I knew I had to get another job quick though because I still needed him to know that I could still maintain with or without his help. So two days later I started filling out job applications everywhere. A week later Smoothie King called me in for an interview. They hired me on the spot and started the very next day. It was a fun job. The 1st time in my life I got to work around white people. Ain't that something? I didn't know any white people on a personal level. Anyway the job didn't pay much but it gave me sense of independence and I enjoyed my work. But that only lasted a few months because I was offered another job with First Union National Bank and I really wanted to work at a more prestigious job with benefits. It was a good job. I was a roving teller, which meant I moved around to different banks and I got to dress in a more professional attire than at Smoothie King.

Things between Raheem and I were going ok I suppose. For the most part I just tried to not to agitate him by questioning him about his whereabouts when he came home at 3 or 4 in the morning. Only because I didn't want to get cursed out or maybe even beat up. I kinda suspected he was still messing around with his baby's momma but I didn't really have any proof. I just always felt uneasy whenever she and I were in the same room. She wasn't what I would call disrespectful towards me or anything but she made her presence known by the way she spoke to him….almost like slick flirting to let me know that he was still checking for her. You know women can be messy for no reason. I don't think she wanted him she just wanted to show me that she still had him in her pocket. So we weren't enemies but we weren't friends. Well anyway around this time we only had occasional arguments but we weren't fighting. He was being nice to me. He bought me a living room set and an entertainment center for my apartment and I was grateful because the sofa I currently had came from a neighbor and it came with roaches. So I was glad to be getting something new.

It was around the time for my birthday and my girl Shanti called asking me what I was gonna do for my birthday and I really didn't know. I wanted to go to this club called 559 because all my friends use to go and I had never been because I know that Raheem would be there and probably be drunk and I didn't want to deal with that. She talked me into going with her and Nale. I meet Shanti though Tela which was Raheem's friend and we immediately connected.

IT'S MY BIRTHDAY

We hung out sometimes going shopping, out to eat or just chillin at my crib or hers, and I met Nale through her. She worked in her hair salon. Little did I know that I would end up working there after I lost my job at the bank because of Raheem. That's another story I'll get back to later. So I agreed to go. I told or more so asked Raheem if I could go and he said yeah baby that's cool, me and my boys gon be there and we all can celebrate your birthday together. I was so excited to be getting out the house for some fun. When we got in the club it was packed. We saw Raheem and his boys over in the corner chopping it up with some chicks so we walked over. Raheem introduced me to a few girls as his lady then he ordered bottles of champagne. We were having a good time listening to the music and Shanti was telling me who was who concerning the females that would come by to speak to their crew.

Shanti and Nale grew up on another side of town so they knew some of everybody. I didn't know anybody. So as I'm listening to them I thought I spotted my cousin Woodie in another section in the club and I told Shanti. I think he spotted me too because a few minutes later he walked up to me with this big kool aid smile and hugged me. He said what's up cuz I ain't seen you in so long. I told him it was my birthday and I was out with my friends and my dude. So he said what ya'll drinking cause I'm bout to buy ya'll whatever ya'll want. I told him we were ok cause my dude had just bought us a bottle of Moet. He said ok you sure cause I got you cuz. I said yeah we good. He saw some chick he knew and said I'm come back in a minute and holla at u cuz happy birthday. Soon as he walked off Raheem walked up and grabbed my arm and pulled me in the corner. He started punching me in my stomach talking about "who is that nigga that was hugging on you?" "I said baby that's my cousin Woodie." So he punches me again and I double over and his boy Shot Caller walked up and said "man what's wrong why you tripping hitting her like that?" Raheem said, "I saw her hugging all up on another nigga." Shot Caller said, "Man that's her cousin. You don't know Woodie from JoyLand and Carver

Homes?"

Raheem said, "I ain't never seen him at no family reunion." I was thinking to myself you ain't never been to one of my family's reunion.

His buddy pulled him away and was talking to him. Shanti came and asked what happened and I told her I was ready to go because I knew he was about to be on some dumb shit. She said ok. So we were standing off to the side and Raheem and his crew walk passed us. As soon as he got in front of me, he elbowed me in my face so hard that I flew backwards into a table and fell. Blood was all over the front of my shirt because he had busted my nose. I ran into the ladies room embarrassed and scared. Seconds later Woodie and his crew burst into the bathroom asking me what the hell was going on? He said we finna go find this nigga and give him the business. I just told him to leave it alone cause I didn't want to start a war between them when I knew in my heart I wasn't gonna stop being with Raheem. So this was the worst birthday ever for me. I knew then I didn't want to go anywhere else with him.

He waited a few days and called and said he was sorry and if he could come over and talk to me. I wanted him to come and at the same time I didn't want him to come. I wanted to know what I had did wrong. Needless to say we got back together after he said he would never do that to me again. I believed him but it turned out he was lying. As a way to show me he was sorry he bought me a car. A white Honda Accord. Things were cool and we were in a good place or so I thought. We went on a double date vacation to Orlando with Shanti and Tela. I had so much fun. We saw all the attractions at Disney World and relaxed at the resort in the pool a lot. Once we got home and I went to work I figured things would be good with us because we had such a great time on our mini vacation. Well he started popping up at my job observing me as I worked. He asked me why I smiled at the men that came into the bank. I told him the same reason I smiled at the women too. It was a part of my job to be professional, and friendly with the customers and it was actually a requirement of my job. He would tell me not to go to work sometimes cause he wanted me to stay home with him.

Eventually I lost that job because I called out too much and I was late a lot. So he was happy about it. It was about a month before I got another job. This time it was with Nale and Shanti at the salon as a receptionist. It worked well for me because I had experience with customer service and I was polite and professional. He started threatening me about the hours I worked and was upset because I couldn't tie up the phone lines talking to him. One night he came home drunk and woke me up out of my steep by grabbing me by my hair saying a dude named Pedro I use to talk to was mugging him in the club and he said the dude told him we still mess around and he knew where I stayed. I knew he was lying because the dude had never been in my apartment, he only knew what building I lived in. I got dressed and went outside with him to see this guy. So we're outside waiting for 10 minutes for this phantom guy to pull up and the guy never showed because he made it all up. Why, I don't know?

Anyway that was another ass whooping I had to take for his imagination and that wouldn't be the last time. When he would fight me it was like he was fighting a man no slaps and pushes. He would punch me in the face with his fist. I was 5'1, a buck 25 soaking wet and he was 6'2 200lbs. he had no business putting his hands on me like that. My girl Rae from way back use to tell me that he was no good for me and to never have a baby by him. I didn't listen because I thought that he would stop beating on me and realize I was good woman. So I stay with him forgiving him each time he put his hands on me. I guess he was good enough for her though because rumors started floating around that they were messing around. I just knew that wasn't true because we were really good friends and she was my girl. Come to find out when I asked her about it she said she wasn't gonna justify me with an answer.

As if I shouldn't even question her about something like

that cause we've been friends for so long. I told her because we've been friends so long she should have no problem answering it. She eventually told me it was her little sister who was messing with him. I said, is this the same little sister I claim as my little sister? We argued about why she didn't tell me. She said I tried to tell you he was no good. I told her as tight as we were she should've told her sister she was wrong. At the end of the day our friendship dissolved because I just didn't believe her. I felt that was something she would take to her grave, she was never gonna admit it was her. I asked him, well I lied to him and told him she fessed up to sleeping with him so he would tell me the truth.

He admitted to sleeping with her and it hurt me so much that I had to go throw up. I still stayed with him. That's how dumb I was. I cut her off like it wasn't his fault too. I should've left his ass then. Well time passed and Rae was upset that I wasn't fooling with her and she made a cassette tape talking about how I use to give her his blow to get high with and things about my past. I never thought in a million years she would do that. I wanted to bust her in her face because I got the hell beat out of me. (Thanks for looking out Rae.) I did give her a little dust here and there because I knew he wouldn't miss it. She made it seem like I was giving her ounces. I didn't do it with her because I didn't want to. I did experiment with it when I was younger way before I met Raheem but he didn't know that. I didn't understand. She slept with my man and was mad at me for not being her friend anymore.

Things got worse from that point on. I recall getting beat up every month for a whole year. Today was beautiful day and it was Freaknik in the A. I lived on Boulevard and all the traffic was on my street. It was mass pandemonium! The street was almost in gridlock. Cars driving by only able to go around 2 miles or so an hour. So me and a few of my friends were sitting out on our car hoods laughing and just enjoying the madness that came with Freaknik. Girls danced on the top of cars, some almost naked. It was so fun just watching and laughing. Anyway

Raheem, Tela and some more of their crew rode down the street in a convertible. We were just chillin having fun. Later that night around 3 am in the morning Raheem called me to come get him from his mom's house. I was asleep and didn't want to get up so I asked him why he didn't get Tela to drop him off. He started cursing telling me to come get him. So I slipped on one of his sweat suits and got Nandi out of bed to bring her with me to go get him.

Once I got to his moms house I got out of the car to get in the passenger seat so he could drive back home. He was coming out the door as I was going around the front of the car and he grabbed me by my neck and started choking me. I was struggling to get a loose because he was so much stronger than I was. He grabbed my chin and the top of my head at the same time and kept trying to twist it like he was trying to break my neck. I was desperately trying to get away from him. I started screaming for help and calling his momma's name. "Ms. Shaw! Help me!" She came outside along with her granddaughter and they were grabbing him trying to make him stop fighting me. His niece started going off on him and he stared trying to fight her. She went and got a knife and said I ain't scared of you I'm gon stab yo ass if you put your hands on me. He told me to take off his clothes. His mom said she ain't taking off a damn thing! You need to bring yo drunk ass in this house and get your self together. We stayed at her house for about 45 minutes.

He was crying and talking about his brother that died when he was 12, it was all so bizarre. Then we left. He started to calm down some on the way home or so I thought. I drove of course. When we got back home he started going off asking me why I had on sweats now cause that ain't what I had on earlier. I said I was in the bed sleep when you called so I got up and slipped these on to come get you. He said but you was looking like a slut earlier today. I said I had on an outfit you picked out so what's the problem? You told me I looked nice today but now I looked like a slut. I knew the bull shit was about to begin again. He started punching me and knocked me unconscious.

When I came to I was lying in the bed with a gown on and a cool rag on my forehead. Nandi was sitting next to me and she said momma you woke up! Raheem was laying on the bed watching tv. I asked him what happened because I didn't remember having on a gown and why was a wet rag on my face. He said you fainted and I couldn't wake you up. I couldn't remember anything but I knew something wasn't right. The next day I called Shanti and she said I hate that bastard Raheem. I asked her what was wrong She said last night he hit you so hard he knocked you out. He called Tela and told him man what I need to do I done knocked this bitch out and I cant wake her up. Tela told him to take you to the hospital. He put you and your baby in the car and drove there but didn't take you in because he was scared they were gonna lock him up so he just brought you back home and put you in the bed with your sleeping clothes on so If you died he could say it happened in your sleep. I was crushed.

What if I hadn't wakened up? I started to resent him more and more everyday and I still didn't leave. I wanted him to love me and realize he had a down ass ride or die chick on his team. I tried really hard to do everything right so he would recognize my efforts and see me, but he never did. It was around that time that God started to reveal Himself to me in ways that I didn't understand and I didn't know how to receive what He was telling me. One night while we were asleep I was awakened by the sounds of murmuring. The house was quiet but the sounds I heard were amazingly loud! I don't know if you've ever heard the phrase "silence is deafening"? It basically means that the absence of noise is so profound that it seems to have its own quality. If that makes any sense to you? Ok how about this, try getting somewhere by yourself one day in a place where there isn't any noise and still yourself and see if you feel what I'm trying to convey to you. Anyway the murmuring woke me up and I looked up at the ceiling and I could see these floating figures that looked like Casper the friendly ghost except they were black and not so friendly looking. They were swarming around bumping into each other with a menacing look on their faces. They were in number of about 12 and they were right above Raheem's side of the bed and it was obvious they were angry! I was terrified! I looked over at him and he was tossing his head back and forth as if he was having a bad dream. I tried shaking him to wake him up but he wouldn't wake up.

I closed my eyes and started praying to God that this can't be real. When I opened me eyes these ghostly figures were gone. He was sleeping peacefully again and I thought maybe I imagined it all but I just couldn't shake the eerie feeling that was all over me. Little did I know that this wouldn't be the last time I experienced something like that. The next morning I wanted to tell somebody but I didn't want people to think I was crazy or that I must've been tripping and had a bad dream. But I know with everything in me it wasn't a dream, it was real and I was feeling troubled about it. I didn't know what it meant. I told Raheem and he just brushed it off. So a little later I called Kel and was telling her about it and she said girl what you experienced was real. "God was trying to tell you something.

What, I don't exactly know but you need to come to church with me tomorrow night. My pastor is a prophet and you need to be in the building. He might have something you need to hear." "I said ok I'll go cause that was just way past weird what I felt." I wasn't a stranger to church. Grew up in church, had been in church all my life but as I was growing into adulthood I sorta got away from it all because in all honesty I didn't understand what the preacher was saying to me when I did go. Raheem and I went sometimes but it was only on occasion. So I called my sister Emon to go with me. I took Nandi too and she was really sick with an ear infection. When we got there the church was crowded and the pastor was giving his sermon. He came out of the pulpit and start engaging with the congregation and that was something that I'd ever saw a pastor do. He started touching people on their heads and they would fall on the floor. I immediately thought it was a show and the people were phony. He was walking all around the church placing his hands on people and it amazed me that they would drop to the floor. It all looked silly to me. I wasn't convinced it was real. He later asked all who needed prayer to come down to the altar. My sister told me to take Nandi down for prayer and I said if he's a prophet then he should know she's sick, I ain't going down there. After the service was over as we were coming out of the church we stood to the side to allow the ministerial team to come by.

The pastor and his staff passed by us and he immediately turn around and came and stood in front of me and said give me the baby. I was shocked and I handed him my baby. He held her little body next to his for a moment, then passed her to one of his ministers and pointed to me and said it ain't the baby, it's you! You don't believe. He placed his hands on my head and shoulder and was saying something that I don't remember because my eyes had closed and when I came to I was on the floor! I didn't know what to believe because I had never experienced anything like that. Yet I still doubted if it was real or not. I went to church with her a few more times and I listened to what he was saying because I needed to know about these mixed feelings I was having. I remember him saying when God tells you to pray you need to stop whatever you're doing and pray right then even if you don't know what to pray for he will give you the words.

If you cant find the words just say Jesus and keep repeating His name and God will hear the things that are in your heart that you cant put into words. That stayed with me. I wasn't really religious but I believed in God. So later that week I was at home alone and I had the water running about to get in the shower. I heard a voice that said, you need to pray. I tried to dismiss it and said as soon as I get out the shower I'll pray. So I wrapped my towel around me and went into to bathroom. I heard the voice again only louder and more of a command saying, pray now! It scared me so I turned off the shower and went into my bedroom and got on my knees and started praying. I didn't even know what I needed to pray for and why I had to so urgently? I didn't know how to pray.

The only people I'd heard praying was pastors and I sure didn't know how to pray like them. I felt like I was gonna sound foolish. So I just started saying what I had heard before.

"Thank you Jesus for my life. Thank you for making my baby well. Thank you for a roof over my head, food on my table and clothes on my back."

It was all what I had heard out of ritual. I didn't know what else to say so I started saying thank you Jesus, thank you Jesus over and over again. Somehow the words just started to spew forth from my mouth and I was thanking God for His mercy and grace and I was praying for homeless people, for people struggling with any and everything. I was praying for Raheem in whatever he was going through. I was lost in prayer to the point that not only was I praying to Jesus I was praising Him! It was like I was having an out of body experience. There was this bright divine light that was surrounding me and I could feel the warmth on my back. In the darkness of my room with my eyes closed I could still see this bright deliberate penetrating glow from this light. It was almost too much for me to comprehend.

I wanted to turn around to gaze on His Majesty and all His glory but I couldn't because of something that I had heard in church as a child about a woman who was turned into a pillar of salt for turning around to look back at something. I didn't know the whole story but I knew I wasn't about to turn around. And everything in me that was spiritual, let me know that it was my Lord right there with me. He came to see about me! This unworthy, undeserving, non-believing, filthy, less than dirt particle of dust. He was with me. I was afraid but more so in a way that acknowledged His presence that I just laid prostrate before Him and declared Him Lord of my life and ruler over everything. I don't know how long I stayed on that floor worshiping. But when I got up I felt like weights had been lifted off of me. I knew that God lived in me and I knew he was there protecting me even when I didn't know it. I never forgot that encounter, and I never will. I knew I had to get closer to God.

There were some good times, but the bad times outweighed any good we had. And no matter how mean he was to me I always prayed for him.

RUN

We eventually moved out of my apartment two years later and into our house. He proposed to me later that year with a $12,000 ring. I thought that was the beginning of better days. The abuse didn't get any better. It kept getting worse. I wanted to leave so bad but I was too scared to. He was so unpredictable. He would get drunk and beat on me and be sober and do the same. His temper was off the charts. One night he had went out with his friends and I was at home just enjoying some me time. Nandi was at my sister's house with her kids at a family sleep over. I took a shower got in the bed and started watching something on tv and before you know it I was asleep. I was awaken by the phone ringing. When I answered it was Shanti saying "Skye! Wake up! I been calling you back to back for five minutes!"

"I said what's wrong?"

"She said you got to get out of the house right now!" "Why? What's wrong Shanti?"

"Raheem was just on the phone with Tela and was telling him when he gets home he is gon beat you so bad."

"For what tho?"

"He was just going on about some dude you use to mess with and Tela was trying to tell him to chill out and that he couldn't get mad about a dude that you was with before him."

"What dude is he talking about?"

"I don't know chile I think Tela said Pedro."

"Girl I get so tired of him with this ancient ass relationship I had with this boy!"

"Girl just get out now man cause he on the way and he is furious!"

"Thanks for the heads up. I'll call you later."

"Get up now Skye!"

"Okay!"

I got up and slipped on some shorts and a tee shirt and some bedroom shoes and I heard the phone ring again. It was Raheem. "You need to get up and get ready to open the door for me, I'll be there in a few minutes."

"Ok are you alright?" He said just get up so you can open the door. I was already dressed so I went and sat on the steps waiting for him to pull up. I had my phone in one hand and keys in my other so I could open the door for him. I could see my purse sitting on the kitchen table from where I sat, why that crossed my mind I didn't know. I started thinking maybe I could talk him out of whatever it was that was bothering him. Then I heard the car pull up and I panicked. I was nervous all of a sudden and I knew I had to get out of there. I heard him unlock the burglar bar door and I knew he had to unlock two locks on the main door before he could come in.

Once I heard the burglar bar open I got up, grabbed my purse off the table and ran down to the garage. I pressed the button to open it and got in my car and pulled off. I knew he wasn't gonna leave either door unlocked and he wasn't gonna leave the garage door open before he gave chase after me so that would buy me a little time. I was flying out of our subdivision. I figured if I made it to Memorial Drive I could get away. No sooner than I thought that, I saw his car swerving in my rear view and heading my way fast. I kept going and when I made it to the main street he was right on my tail. I was in and out of lanes, running red lights and flashing my high beams to get somebody's attention. I came upon a light that had too many cars for me to run it so I had to stop.

Raheem swerved his car in front of mine attempting to block me in. He got out of his car and started running towards my car. I was looking at him coming towards me and it felt like this was happening in slow motion. I almost laughed inside because he looked so retarded. I put my car in reverse and backed back in between two other cars then I went around his car and sped down the street. I saw him almost hit a car from my rearview mirror as he tried to catch up to me. I kept going, still flashing my headlights, hoping to alert a police officer since we were right down the street from the Dekalb County Jail. I was in disbelief that I hadn't seen not one police car. Any other time if I had been speeding down that street I would've been pulled over and given a ticket. He was still chasing after me and I decided to head toward the jail and maybe he would turn the other way. But that didn't happen. I drove into the jails parking lot and he followed behind me.

I circled around and drove down to the docks where they bring arrested people in. He followed me down there too. I knew then that this idiot had no respect for the law. I came around the back entry and headed back up to the entrance of the jail. I was about to drive up on the grass in front of their doors to get somebody's attention when I saw a police car approaching and I started flashing my lights at him. He turned on his blue lights and pulled up towards my car. Do you believe that this clown Raheem had the nerve to pull up beside my car? You would think that he would've just pulled off to keep from having to speak to the police officer but he just sat there. The officer walked to my car and I rolled down my window. What seems to be the problem ma'am? I started to explain to him the ordeal that had just taken place when a cab that was nearly run off the road by Raheem earlier pulled up and got out of his car in hysterics! He was Ethiopian I believe. His dialect was of African descent. He said "lock that jackass up Mr. Police Man! He nearly ran me off the road chasing this young lady down the street. He was very reckless in his driving sir. I followed him all the way down here and I want to press charges on him for almost killing me!" The officer said sir just get back in your vehicle and I will get a statement from you in a moment.

So I said that's what I was telling you officer. He is crazy. He has to be to follow me inside the jail premises. He told me to sit there and he was going over to talk to Raheem. I called Shanti and told her the whole story and she was laughing and saying that boy is retarded for real. They ended up locking him up that night for DUI and reckless driving. I guess he called his niece at some point because she got there and told me Raheem said give her my house keys because I had to get out. I laughed and told her to get her stupid ass out my face. I wasn't giving her shit. This is where I live. So because he acts stupid I gotta get out. I don't think so. The officer told her that he can't make me leave if that's where I've been residing without a thirty days notice. I was glad they locked him up because if he had gotten to me he was definitely gonna hurt me.

He was so stupid. Who does stuff like that?......Have a high speed chase with your girlfriend? I went home and got back in the bed. I didn't know what was gonna happen tomorrow and I didn't care. I was tired and I just wanted to go to sleep. Again, time went on and we still stayed together. I wasn't happy all the time, but everyday wasn't a bad day either. I got pregnant and I was devastated! I didn't want his baby. That meant I was gonna have to deal with him for the rest of my life and I was discouraged behind that thought. We found out it was a boy and he was happy. The beatings ceased for a while. He did get mad at me one day for something I cant clearly remember but he grabbed my stomach and squeezed it hard instead of hitting me. I was five months pregnant with his son and he did not care. Later that week as a way to try to make up for what he did he asked me what did I want to do for my birthday.

Of course I had a flash back of what had taken place a few years before, so I said I really hadn't thought about doing anything for my birthday being so pregnant and all. So he said let's go somewhere then. Anywhere you want to go we can go. So I said I wanna go to Hawaii. He said ok and we made the travel arrangements the next day. Two weeks later we were in Honolulu Hawaii. It was beautiful there. I loved the exotic flowers, the music and the golden glow on the skin of the islanders. The people were friendly and full of smiles. I had the pleasure of wading through the waters in the Pacific Ocean and walking through an inactive volcano. We stayed there for four days enjoying the sites and eating the freshest seafood I'd ever tasted. Then we flew to another island called Kauai and stayed there for three more days. This island was more secluded and laid back we watched dolphins jumping in and out the water while having lunch at a local restaurant there. Their stray chickens walking through the streets was as normal as stray dogs roaming the streets of Atlanta.

It was so interesting to witness how different our cultures were. I had never been to Hawaii and I felt blessed to be there. That was one of the good times. We had visited other places before. Miami, Las Vegas, New York, Biloxi and the Bahamas! None of these places compared to Hawaii. We returned home and I was still feeling good. Things seemed to go well in our relationship. He didn't put his hands on me for a long time. I guess because I was so big and pregnant. He would buy me nice jewelry and clothes or anything I wanted at any given time, but mostly I felt like he did it as a way of apologizing for fighting me. I had a lot of both, so you know that means I wore a lot of butt whippings. One night we were asleep and I was awaken by a sound that I was frighteningly familiar with. It was a sound that I would never forget from a past experience. It was the same murmuring I'd heard from years before. I was 8 months pregnant and barely able to move but I sat up in the bed quickly. I looked up at the ceiling and it was covered with the same black figures that it was before. Only this time it was too many to count and they were still only covering his side of the room. I would've screamed if I could've found my voice but I couldn't. Not only were there these ghosts but there was another type of evil that presented itself. There was this midget looking monster with jagged teeth that was murmuring while walking towards me and it seemed that it was taking him a long time to get there but he was coming!

I thought I was going to black out or something because I felt so weak. I started screaming "Jesus! Jesus! Help me!" I knew this was bigger than me and the only help I knew that could handle something like this was Jesus. You would've thought Raheem would wake up as loud as I was screaming Jesus' name and praying but he was lying there jerking around in his sleep. I knew then whatever it was, was after him and not me. It wouldn't be much longer before God removed me from this horror story I was living. I had our son in June. When I came home from the hospital my best friend Kel came with me to help me get settled in. I laid my baby down on our bed and I noticed a long curly strand of hair on the bed. I asked Kel was this her hair and she said no. So I'm wondering whose is it because it damn sho ain't mine. I said "I know this dude ain't brought no broad to our house." Kel said "chill man it's probably his sisters. You've been in the hospital for 6 days and his sister could've just been straightening up for you". I was like yeah you right he wouldn't bring no chick here, hell he don't even want none of my friends here.

A month later him and his crew threw a big picnic at South Bend Park like they did every year so the baby and I went. Nandi was with her girl cousins at a sleepover. It was good to be outside and not pregnant. It was packed! Everybody was there. I was cooling with my girls as they were admiring my pretty little baby. I didn't stay long because I was breastfeeding and lil Raheem was starting to get a little fussy. I got home and fed him, took a shower, and started getting ready for bed. I was exhausted. The next few months came and went without incident. He told me he knew a girl that told him about this opportunity to invest in this daycare for $20,000. So we went to check it out. One night, I was at his mom's house, and the phone rang, and I answered it. This girl asked to speak to Raheem. I said whose calling. She said Salina. So I said the girl with the daycare proposition? She said yes. I had some business I needed to ask him about. I asked her why was she calling for him so late for a business issue? And what was so important that it couldn't wait until in the morning? I'm the CFO so can I help you with something? She said you're right I'll just call him back in the morning and she hung up. Something didn't feel right about her call so I called her back. "Hey Salina, this is Skye Raheem's girlfriend. You just called for him a few minutes ago, and I'm calling you back because I just feel like it's more to what's going on between you two than this business venture." "She said no it's just that. I only wanted to run something by him that's all." "I don't believe you. So, I'm gonna say this, woman to woman, if he was your man and I was doing what you are doing with him, how would you feel?" At first, she was still sticking to her story and I said "ok if that's what you want me to believe cool but just know that its all fun and games until he's your man and you have kids with him and he does the same disrespectful shit to you that he's doing to me.

The same way he's sneaking and doing stuff with you is the same way he'll do it with somebody else." I guess that registered in her mind and she started spilling the beans. She told me that they had sex at his moms house and on the boat at Lake Lanier. When he took her shopping at the Versace store she picked a few items out for me too. She then told me that while I was in the hospital recovering from having my son that she stayed at the house and had sex with him there too. I told her I didn't believe her because he was really particular about who came over because he knew anybody could set you up to be robbed. So I knew for sure she was lying about being in my house. Then she started describing my clothes and shoes in my closet. She described things that were under my bathroom cabinet and the furniture throughout the house. She said she had straightened up around the house for me and that she washed some of my clothes, folded them up and put them in the laundry basket. Then she kinda chuckled and said, "I was like why she got all these big panties?"

I knew she was telling the truth about being in my house. I was so hurt but I couldn't let her know that. So I asked her if she has ever been pregnant and she said no. Well if you had, you would know the further along you go in your pregnancy the bigger everything gets and to be comfortable the little cute panties don't work. But had you taken the time out while you were snooping in my shit to look in the second drawer of my night stand you would've found all the pretty Victoria Secrets matching bra and panties in over flow. Please believe I stay laced in the finest but I don't have to tell you that cause you've been all in my closet. That little Versace shit you picked out for me was nothing. Bitch I got a vast Versace collection, sweat suits, shoes, bags, pants shirts, a $3000 coat and at least 8 dresses, belts, sunglasses and jewelry. All Versace. Not to mention the Ralph Lauren and Jones New York business suits and a gang of other overly expensive shoes and shit that he bought. Plus my children stay sponsored by Ralph Lauren and that Coogi shit too. But like I said you already know that cause you've been in my house. "How did you feel sleeping on my Polo sheets and looking up at that big 24X30 picture of us hanging over our bed?"

She didn't say anything but I knew she felt stupid. But so did I. She apologized for what she did and said that she truly knows one day she was gonna have to pay for it because it would probably happen to her. After I got of the phone with her all kinds of things started to run through my mind but what stood out the most was months ago when I came home from the hospital and I saw that strand of hair on our bed. I knew I wasn't crazy. I just couldn't understand why he would bring another woman into our home. He could've gone to her place or any hotel but I guess that was who he was and he really didn't give a damn. I went home and waited for him to get there.

When he got there I asked him what was up with him and Salina and he said man we just business partners. "So now you fuck your business partners?" "Man what are you talking about?" "She told me everything stupid! You fucked her in our bed? You fucked her at your momma house and at the lake? You so nasty and disrespectful! I hate you so much. Why? Just tell me why? You give me hell about any little thing, but you do everything and it's suppose to be ok?" He just said he was sorry and he was just stupid and he was not messing with her anymore. "No shit!? That's just because you got found out." I just walked off to go get my baby because I heard him crying and he probably needed to be changed. I can't even explain what I'm feeling right now other than crushed. I wanted to leave but I didn't have anywhere to go and I was too embarrassed to let anyone of my friends know what was going on. I knew I had to leave but I had to have a plan first.

After that he started buying me all kinds of shit that I didn't need nor did I want. He came home with a platinum bracelet and some diamond earrings. They were beautiful but they didn't change the way I felt. I just added them to my collection of "I'm sorry for fucking you over gifts." Our lives continued on. We would go out to eat dinner with friends, go to movies or over to his relatives homes for special occasions like birthdays or anniversaries. I always wore a smile because some days were better than others and I didn't want people to know I was silently suffering inside from mental, emotional and physical abuse at the hands of someone who said they loved me. I loved having the kids around because it made me happy to see them having so much fun with each other. They would run through the house laughing hysterically at each other or play with their toys together. Blood couldn't have made them more related. We didn't get to see Shelby that often because she lived in Griffin Ga. with her mom but Chayla would be there on weekends sometimes and I loved having them there.

It seemed like Raheem was less likely to insult me or fight me when the kids were around. They loved their little brother to pieces! They were all so small and thought they were big enough to hold him. So I had to take turns propping them up on the sofa with pillows so they could hold him. They were never trying to out do one another. They were as all kids are so innocent in their love. It was getting close to Christmas and we had finished all the shopping for the kids. Our Christmas tree was decorated so lavishly that it looked like a Macy's tree. Whatever I wanted for the house or the kids or for myself Raheem got it. Him and his boys were throwing a Christmas ball at the Crown Hotel on Virginia Ave. Everybody was talking about it and who was gonna be in the building and what they were gonna wear. Raheem and I went to Phipps Plaza to the Versace store to get our gear because we had to be on point cause all eyes were gonna be on us. He bought me a maroon ball gown that was $1300 along with the matching shoes that were $700. His matching suit was about $2100. We were ballin baby! Four days later he called me and said go see Big Joe in Green Briar Mall because he had something for me. I had my mom with me out running errands so I was like ok. When I got there Joe was like hi lovely how are you. I said I'm fine how are you Joe? He said fat and happy while rubbing his huge belly. I laughed cause he was a lil fat Italian man. He said "I just got these alligator shoes in check them out and let me know if you like them." So I took a look at them and said "I like the black ones." "He said ok which other ones you like?" "I said the gold ones are nice."

THAT BOY CRAZY ABOUT YOU

He said, “Ok what size do you wear?” “I said a six.” He told Danny who worked in the store to go get my size. I was looking at the prices on the shoes cause I knew alligator shoes were expensive. The ones I told him I liked were $800! He then asked me what else I liked and I looked at him and said I like all of them but they cost a lot of money. He said “keep picking cause you got six pair all already paid for by your husband.” I was smiling from ear to ear. So I picked out four more pair. That was a ridiculous amount of money to spend on those shoes. Danny got all my shoes together and started packing them up. Joe then said “come with me to the back Skye.” So I followed him and he pulled out a full floor length black mink coat. He told me to try it on. It fit perfectly!

I modeled it in the three way mirror and said, "This is a beautiful coat Joe.” He said, “Good, I’m glad you like it because its yours too.” I all but fell out back there. The coat was $10,000! He said “that man must sure enough love you. He just spent a lot of money in here on you today.” I was ecstatic! We left out of the mall with Danny as my security guard and I needed him because my mom and I couldn’t tote all those bags. People were staring at us like we were celebrities or something. Danny made sure we were good and waved goodbye as I pulled off still smiling. My momma said “that boy crazy about you! He sent you in that store and had already paid for everything?" I told her he could be sweet like that sometimes. I had to give him credit, that was some real playa shit he did. I dropped my mom off at home and headed home myself. Once Raheem got there I had already put my new things away and was almost done with dinner. I made some barbeque chicken, mac and cheese, cabbage and cornbread. He walked in and was on his phone talking but he said something smells good. I said me and laughed. When he finished his conversation he came in the kitchen looking like he hadn’t just spent damn near $20,000 on me I went up to him and threw my arms around his neck and kissed him and thanked him for all my gifts. I said “baby that was so sweet of you. I really appreciate my things. I’m about to be crushing these hoes!" He started laughing and said "you been crushing them hoes baby. I can't be around here with this kind of gear and not have my lady looking like me." "I said you right baby" and thanked him again. He said, "When is the food gone be ready cause I'm hungry and where my boy at?"

"The food ready I'm about to pull the cornbread out the oven now. Your son is upstairs taking a nap so please don't wake him up."

He said, "Ok" I knew he was gonna go right up there and start kissing on him and wake him up. It was moments like this that helped me remember why I wanted our family to work, not because of the things he did for me but because he could be such a caring man and he loved his children. I wished it could always be this way. When he was being loving and considerate it made it harder for me to leave because I saw a different side of him.

I thought this side of him would overpower the evil in him where Satan took up residence, but I guess it was really hard for him to resist the devil. I grew up in church so I believed that there was good in everyone and as far as Raheem was concerned it was my Christian duty to show him as much love as I could while enduring the turbulence of our relationship. I was right but I was foolish in accepting his abuse, but at that time I didn't know any other way to love him other than not to desert him. It was the night of the party and we were getting dressed. He looked really handsome and I was looking like royalty! We took a limousine there and when we arrived the place was decorated very elegantly. All eyes were on us as we were the host of the party. I was seated at the VIP table with his mom, sisters, niece and some of Tela's family and Shanti. She was FLAWLESS and more than likely sponsored by Gucci cause Tela kept her fly. We were all drinking champagne and talking jamming to the music when Kot and Monicia came in and Raheem introduced me to her and they sat at the table and started cutting up with us.

We were having a ball. Later Javin Puri and Ragged End

came in and the party was in full force. Then the DJ said this song is for the lady and man of the hour so Raheem you and Skye come on out here and take the floor for your first dance. I felt so special. He took my hand and lead me to the dance floor. As he embraced me we danced to K-Ci and Jojo All My Life. As everyone watched us dancing I felt like the luckiest girl in the room. He was spinning me around and dipping me back over his arm and singing to me. As I looked into his eyes I saw the man that I had fallen in love with. The song ended and he kissed me. Everyone clapped. The music started back up and people came back on the floor to dance.

We went back to our table and Shanti and I was slapping high fives and laughing. She said "if these broads fronting like they didn't know who you was before, make no mistake about it they know now!" So anyway as the night went on we mingled with people and took pictures. People were coming by our table speaking and a group of dudes from my hood walked passed and spoke to us. Some said hello, I simply threw up my hand.

The night was going perfect and we had started making plans to not let it end there. We were going to Club 112 after we left there. We were leaving out of the club and Shanti and I were laughing and talking to some more friends ready to go to the club. We were standing outside now just talking about how much fun we had and Raheem was talking to JP and the crew but he turned around and told me to go get in the limo. I ask him why cause we were all standing around talking to each other. So he said just go get in the car. So I hugged my friends necks and said see ya'll in a minute we bout to go shut the club down! I hugged his sisters and mom and said I would see them later. I got in the limo and was sitting there about 20 minutes looking out the window as everyone else was still talking and laughing with each other. I felt left out.

Finally Raheem got in the limo. He asked me did I have a good time and I said I had the time of my life thank you baby.

He said, "Did you see DooDoo them when they came in.?"

I said, "No but they did walk pass our table and spoke."

"Oh so he spoke to you?"

I said, "No they all said hi and your sister them spoke and I threw up my hand."

"So you just gon disrespect me like that and speak to that nigga you use to fuck with?"

" Raheem I didn't disrespect you. I never even opened my mouth. He didn't speak to me, they said hey as they were passing the table."

"But I'm just saying I just spent damn near $20,000 on you and you talking to a nigga you use to fuck with.?"

"Raheem I was 15 years old when I messed with him. I'm 26 now so that was 11 years before I ever met you. I was a child. I cant even remember the last time I've seen him and I don't care. The last I heard he been in prison for the last 6 or 7 years."

"Oh so you been keeping up with the nigga?"

"No but that's just the streets talking and I'm sure even you know that. Baby we just had one of the best nights of my life, and I want to go to 112 to keep it going."

He said, "We ain't going nowhere but home," and he punched me so hard in my stomach that I lost my breath and doubled over on the floor. He called me all kinds of bitches and hoes. He said that I disrespected him after all he had did for me. And grabbed me up off the floor and started punching me again. Then he started biting my hair out in chunks! I somehow got away from him and was on the other side of the limo begging him not to do this. Then I started beating on the partition that separated us from the driver screaming for him to help me. He didn't. He just kept driving like he didn't hear me back there crying. Raheem stopped but said when we get home he was gonna beat me to death. When we pulled up at home I got out of the car and picked up my shoes of the floor, somehow they had came off during the whole fiasco. I walked past the driver's door and looked back at him and mouthed "please help me." He just pulled off as if it wasn't his place to intervene.

As I walked down the driveway It was like I was looking at the house for the first time. Burglar bars were on all the windows and doors. I had no way to escape my fate, I was gonna get beat to death like he said. True to his word, once we entered the house I only had time to take off my gown and he stared swinging. I ran into the hallway bathroom and he came in behind me and started throwing everything on the counter at me that was within his reach. I was screaming as I was getting hit with the bar of soap, the soap dish, toothbrush holder, brushes, and combs. I was begging him to stop. When he ran out of things to throw, he turned on the sink faucet and was throwing handfuls of water at me. I tried to run out of the bathroom and slipped on the floor. He turned around and kicked me in my back with them hard ass gator shoes and I started bleeding.

I got up and ran into my daughter's room and fell to my knees and started praying. I asked God to please forgive him because he didn't know what he was doing. I didn't ask God to save me nor stop him from hitting me.

He walked in the room and said, "I don't know what you praying to God for, He cant save you."

Then he grabbed me by my hair and dragged me down the hall back towards our room then he let me go. I went back into he hallway bathroom and stuff was everywhere. I didn't even want to look at myself in the mirror as I started to clean the bathroom up by putting things back in its proper place. Then I wiped up all the water up off the floor. I went into our bedroom and he was laying back on the bed with his hand propped up behind his head watching tv. I walked in our bathroom and closed the door so I could take a shower. My hair was all over the place.

My stockings were torn and ripped. As I got into the shower the water was comforting after all the hits I had taken. I let the water run through my head as clumps of hair was falling on the shower floor so I started shampooing it and more of it started to come out as I massaged my scalp. I cried silently in the shower because I didn't want him to hear me. After I got out and dried off, sat on the toilet and combed my hair. More fell out. I finally got the courage to look into the mirror and saw that my face was swelling up and the bruise under my eye had started to darken. I had bald patches in random spots all over my head. I looked at myself and mouthed in the mirror "you are so stupid, you deserved it. You should've just got in the damn car when he told you to! Now you see what your big mouth gets you?

You're so stupid!" After I got out of the shower and came in to put on pajamas he made me lay on the bed and proceeded to put his mouth on my yoni. It felt so nasty! Then he had sex with me. I just laid there like Sealy on The Color Purple and pretend I'm not there and just let mister do his business. He moaning and groaning like this the best he's ever had. I don't say a word because I know......he just raped me. He finally finished and I go get back in the shower in the hottest water my body can stand without melting off and I try to scrub all of him off of me. Now I have red welts all over me in addition to the bruises.

When I came back in the room and put on pajamas he told me to go get him something to drink. I thought I mumbled to myself you been laying her all this time you coulda went and got it yourself, but he heard me and said, "You must've forgot what just happed happened? It ain't nothing for me to beat yo ass again." I didn't say anything I just went to get him something to drink. I wanted to spit in it but I didn't because even with him being as mean to me as he was it just wasn't in my character to do something that nasty. The next day I was sore all over. It felt like I had got jumped in a gang. I had purple bruises all over me. I called Shanti after he left the house and asked her if she knew someone who could braid my hair. She said, "I just did your hair yesterday what's wrong with it and why ya'll didn't come to 112 last night? We had a ball!"

"He changed his mind but give me the girls number cause I want to see if she can do it today."

"What's wrong Skye? What did that bastard do to you?"

"Girl I can't even fix myself to talk about it right now." "Uma give you this girl number but I'm going with you cause you don't sound right." I said "ok," took the number and called the girl to make an appointment. She said she could take me right now because her morning was open and she didn't have anyone scheduled until 3:30 that afternoon. I got there at 10am and Shanti got there about 30 minutes after I did. I was sitting in the chair and the African lady was speaking in her native tongue while she was trying to decide where to start at on my hair. I know they were talking about me because the other lady came over and looked at my head and said something to her and sucked her teeth and walked off. Shanti walked over and I was holding my head down as the stylist was opening a package of braiding hair. "What the fuck happened to your hair?"

I looked up and she just put her hand over her mouth and her eyes looked like they were gonna pop out of their sockets. "Oh my God Skye!"

"I said I didn't know what else to do with my hair cause it had so many bald spots and I thought braids was the safest way to go.

"Look at your damn face and your eye! What is wrong with Raheem? You should've called the police on him. What happened? Ya'll look like ya'll was having so much fun last night."

"Yeah I thought we was too until we got in the limo."

"What could've made him this mad that he would fuck up your face like this?"

"You know it don't take much for him to act a fool. He said I disrespected him by speaking to some guys from my hood. Well

DooDoo to be exact."

"DooDoo? You talking about the boy you use to talk to when you were like 14 or 15?"

"Yeah that pedophile."

"Oh my God ain't he been locked up for some years?"

"Yep."

"Raheem need his ass kicked for that. I can't stand him. Ain't no good gone come to him for the way he treat you."

"Yeah that's wishful thinking cause it seem like he stay on top. I got this camera can you take some pictures of my head? I don't know why I want them but they may come in handy one day.

" "Yeah I'll take them.

Girl your hair was pass your shoulders. That baby grew it out so long and now you got patches of your scalp showing. He gon end up killing your ass if you don't leave him." I didn't say anything because I thought the same thing. I pulled up my shirt and showed her the bruises there and the spot where he kicked me. I had a band aid on it because it was cut there. She just shook her head. She stayed there with me the 3 hours it took to get my hair done and then we left. I told her I would call her later. I was on my way to pick up my kids from my mom's and I really wasn't feeling well. I was sore from the fight and I had a splitting headache. When I got there I just pulled up and called my mom and told her to bring the kids out so we could leave. When she came out with the kids I made sure I had on my shades so she couldn't my eye. I told her thank you for watching them for me. She said anytime sweetie. "What's wrong you usually hang around and talk with me for a little while before you leave."

"I said I just got my hair braided and my head hurts so I just wanted to go home and take something and lay down for a while."

She said "ok baby I'll talk to you later."

Once I got home and put the baby bag down I pulled the shades off. Nandi said she was hungry and wanted some cereal so I fixed them for her and made the baby a bottle. I took some ground beef out so I could make spaghetti later for dinner. She went in her room and asked me to turn on the Disney channel so she could watching tv and eat. I told her to be careful and put a towel down on the floor in case she accidentally spilled her cereal. She looked at me and said "Mommy who hurt your eye?"

"I said mommy is ok watch your show baby."

She said "Did daddy hurt your eye?"

I said, "No honey mommy made a mistake by pulling something off the top shelf in the cabinet and something fell down and hit mommy in the eye."

She didn't say anything she just asked me to turn up the tv and kept eating her cereal.

I got up to walk out and she said," Mommy let me kiss it and make it all better." I leaned in and she did ever so gently and I said, "Thank you baby it feels so much better."

She smiled and I walk out hoping she always stayed that innocent. I took two Tylenol extra strength and bathe lil Raheem and then feed him because he had drank his bottle. He was so precious and cute. I massaged baby lotion on him and sprinkled baby powder on him. I loved when he smelled like that.

After I dressed him, I checked on Nandi and told her it was time for her to take a bath, so bring your bowl downstairs when you finish. She said "ok mommy." I put the baby in his playpen with a few toys and turned on the tv. I went upstairs and ran Nandi a bath with lots of bubbles. I told her ten minutes and that's it. She laughed and said ok. By the time she was done with her bath I was almost finished with dinner. I closed the oven door after I pull the garlic bread out and grabbed the baby then went to help Nandi put on lotion and get in her pajamas. It was 7:30 pm and I had the kids bathed and dinner cooked. I was beyond tired but a mother's work is never done. I told Nandi to come sit in my room and watch tv so she could keep an eye out on the baby while he was in his walker so I could take a quick shower.

As I stood under the hot water from the shower it soothed my aching muscles and I stared to weep because I was searching my mind for what I could have done differently so this wouldn't have happened. I couldn't come up with an answer because I didn't know what I'd done wrong. I played with the kids for a while and then Nandi ended up falling asleep in my bed. I picked her up and laid her in her bed. Gave the baby a warm bottle and he was knocked out 10 minutes later. I soon dozed off and was awaken by the ringing of the phone. "Hello?" "Did you cook something, or do I need to stop to get food?" Raheem asked. "I cooked some spaghetti and garlic bread." He said, "I don't want no spaghetti so I'll just get me some wings." I said," ok" and he hung up the phone.

My stomach growling made me aware that I hadn't eaten and I did want spaghetti. So I fixed me a small plate and put the food up because that was fa sho tomorrow's dinner. I was still tired so I went back upstairs to lay down but ended up folding up the baby's clothes that I had washed 2 days ago. I was putting a tee shirt of Raheem's in his drawer that had somehow made it in the baby's clothes I'd wash and I noticed a piece of paper in the drawer. It was a check for $700 for Salina Brown. I was wondering what he was doing with it. It was dated for December and he said he wasn't messing with her anymore after we got into it about her. He got home around 11:45. I asked him about the check and he said he had cashed it for her.

"So she can't get her own check cashed?"

"Man that shit ain't even that serious."

"It is when you said you didn't mess with her anymore months ago and this check is dated for December. Since it's been that long you won't mind when I deposit into my account."

He said, "No the hell you're not." You would think after all he did to me that putting that lil check in my account would mean nothing to him but he was petty like that. It wasn't that I needed it, I just wanted to feel like I had some kind of rank against a female that he fucked around on me with but I guess I didn't. He couldn't even let me feel like I had a little bit of vindication and on top of that he didn't miss the money because he never even deposited the check. I said, "Really? It's cool."

TOUCH NOT MY ANOINTED

So I got in the bed and went to sleep. The next morning I got up and started washing and folding clothes. Shanti called and asked if I wanted to take the kids to see Disney on Ice at the Fox Theatre. I said that would be cool and we would be ready at six. The house was clean so I didn't have to hear Raheems's mouth about this or that when he didn't lift a finger to even put his clothes in the dirty clothes hamper sometimes. The Disney on Ice was show was really good and the kids were entertained the whole time. By the time I'd gotten them home they were beyond tired and so was I. I put them to bed and poured myself a glass of merlot. I just needed to unwind because those kids had given me a run for my money. I took a shower and started reading a book called "Family" written by my favorite author J. California Cooper. It was a story of a family with a history of generational slavery.

I love to read. At any given time you could find me with my face glued to a book. I just know I'm gonna be writer for somebody's magazine one day. The next day I was helping Raheem pack his luggage for a trip to Baltimore. He was going there to negotiate a record deal for his rap group Goon Nation. They had a very popular single that was in heavy rotation in the south called Goon Life and the video was released a few months ago. They had a heavy following and everybody was excited and hopeful that this group would be among the ones that made it out of the hood. This meeting was important and I hope he knew how to represent himself well and this dream of his came true. This could be the beginning of something that he could never imagine. The life of a hustler could be done with. He said to me, "baby this is it! We about to be rich!" He had to meet with the A&R rep for Columbia Records. HardFace. They said he was a no nonsense businessman and he took his job serious. Raheem was gonna be gone for four days and I was glad about it and I was hopeful that this would work out for him. I may even miss his ugly butt……SIKE!

Man I'm so tired of walking on eggshells in my own

house. Well technically it's in his name so it's his but you know what I mean. I don't plan on doing nothing but chilling the whole time he's gone. Kella wanted me to come pick her up so she can stay over a few days to help me with the kids. That's cool with me because that means I can sleep late and I know that she gon make sure they eat and they are watched.

Raheem called and said he won't be back today because all flights coming out of Baltimore have been canceled due to a severe snowstorm so he says he doesn't know when he'll be able to leave. I asked him how did the meetings go and he said he and rep got into an argument and he didn't know what was gon happen. I told him an opportunity like this doesn't come everyday so he should try to arrange another meeting so there won't be any misunderstandings. He said I ain't finna do shit. I ain't kissing no nigga ass. He was slurring when he said it so I knew he had been drinking. "I don't need you telling me how to run my business anyway. I don't give a fuck about non of that. I'll be home tomorrow. Since you telling something, tell me when the last time you talked to Rod?" "To tell you the truth I don't know when the last time I talked to him. He goes through my mom when he wants to know about Nandi or when he has something for her."

"Yeah bitch you a lie. You just talked to him the other day cause you told me he had got some clothes for Nandi."

"I told you he left some clothes with my mom for her and he told her to ask me to call him."

"See I know you be with that sneaky shit. You think I'm stupid? I know you be still fucking with that nigga."

"Nah I don't think you stupid but I do think you crazy. You don't believe that. You just drunk, trying to start an argument for nothing."

"I'm gone show you how crazy I am when I get back home. You think I beat yo ass the last time? This time I'm beat you to death!" I just asked him why he always gotta find a reason to want to fight? "He said you heard what I said and hung up the phone."

I could find no sleep that night. All night I tossed and turned because I couldn't get it out of my head that he was more ready to come home to beat me than he was to get out of the snowstorm. I remember having this feeling that I just couldn't shake that whole night. It was if I was trying to prepare myself for the inevitable. He was going to hurt me when he got home. I prayed that it was just the liquor talking and he would forget about it. I prayed that he would stop putting his hands on me, hell I prayed that the snow wouldn't let up and he'd be stuck another day. That was a horrible night for me and I cried because I just didn't feel like getting beat up again. I was so tired of being scared of him and living in fear.

I don't remember morning coming because it felt like the night was never going to end. But when I woke up, I jumped up! It was almost like I had been pushed out of the bed. There was a feeling of urgency that told me I had to leave right then. So I went down stairs and grabbed all the trash bags I could find. I woke Kella up and told her get up and help me pack my stuff. I was frantic! I knew I had to leave then or he was going to kill me when he made it back home. I started emptying clothes out of my drawers and taking clothes out of my closet as fast as I could because I didn't know when he would arrive but I had to be gone when he did. I told Kella to go into my daughter's room and put all her stuff in the bags. She said, "What's going on? Why you packing all of your stuff?" "Just do what I asked you to do so we can go." I got all of Lil Raheem's clothes and other belongings and packed them in the truck along with my things that I'd been back and forth to the car with. The truck was filled with so many clothes and shoes that we had to make a second trip to get it all.

Once I got all of our belongings Kella said, "What about your tv's and furniture? Ain't you gon get you stuff."

I said "I don't want any of it. He can keep it all. I just

want to make sure I have all our clothes and my jewelry." I did a once over and we were leaving out of the door when my phone rang. It was him. "What you doing?"

I said, "nothing about to take Kella home."

"Oh okay man my head hurting like hell. I don't know much Hennessy I drunk last night. Now the news people talking about the airport shut down and it might be a day or so before they get any flights out. It's so many people sleeping on the floor inside the airport it's a shame. I'm glad I'm in a room." I was just holding the phone. He said, "Well baby I guess I'll be home when this snow let up." I said, "Okay" and hung up the phone. He called right back and said, "Why you hang up on me?"

"I got my purse and the baby in the car seat trying to put him in the truck and it was either hang up or drop my baby."

"Oh I thought you were trying to be funny."

"Why?"

"Cause of what we talked about last night."

"Oh yeah, you did say you were gonna beat me to death."

"I'm just saying I don't know why you had a baby by that nigga anyway. You knew I was gon come into your life."

I was like you really are tripping. "So I'm just suppose to automatically know you were gonna be in my life?" He said "yeah." I said, "okay let me get this girl home cause this lil boy in the truck showing out."

He said, "Ok I love you."

I said, "Ok bye" and hung up the pone. He didn't call back and if he had I wasn't gonna answer. I drove off in a daze.

What did I just do? Where did I think I was going? Maybe he was just drunk and just talking. I know one thing I wasn't gon wait around to see. I went to Nandi's elementary school and withdrew her. She was asking why she gotta leave school early. I told her we were moving. "Why we moving mommy?" I said "just sit back and chill out. You want some McDonalds?" "Yes! And can I have a vanilla milkshake? And tell them I don't want no onions on my hamburger cause they put onions on it the last time and I told you to tell them I didn't want no onions cause I'm allergic to onions. And tell them I'm a girl! They gave me Inspector Gadget last time and they was suppose to give me a Furbie cause Furbie's is for girls and Inspector Gadget is for boys and I'm a girl not a boy!" I laughed and said "girl if you don't shut up and we ain't even made it to McDonalds yet."

Kella was cracking up laughing, "Saying baby if they don't give her a Furbie! And they better not put no onions on her burger cause miss honey gone read, write, and erase them!" I had to admit it was so funny because she was so animated just like her daddy and she was serious. Her daddy would always describe situations by referencing everybody as "the boy." He was telling me this story one time. "The boy call me talking reckless on the phone bout he on the way with the birds and said that the other boy was with him." I said, "Fuck nigga I don't know what the hell you talking bout no damn birds you must got the wrong number sir. Then he gon try to clean it up and said I meant the bird baths you ordered for your yard and he got the other boy with him….. You know the boy with the girlfriend that be stealing out all them people stores?"

"Skye you know who I'm talking bout? The big booty red girl that be dressing up like nurses and funeral home directors and shit so the people won't be looking at her crazy like she stealing."

"Cause she be looking like she ain't stealing, but she be stealing all them people shit. I told that boy that girl going to jail she keep fucking round with them people stuff."

"….But that ain't what I'm talking bout I just was trying to get you to remember the boy. But anyway I told the other boy to keep that janky ass boy from round me cause I find out he playing with my money its gon be some problems." I was confused ass hell! Just like you. "Rod who the hell is the boy?????" That's what I meant by she was animated just like him. Anyway I dropped them at my moms house and unloaded the rest of our stuff then I called Soni to come follow me to Raheem's mom's house.

When we pulled up at her house I told Soni I would be right back. I rang the doorbell and his mom came to he door. "Hey baby come on in what's wrong?" I guess she could tell something was up because I was looking rough as hell. My ponytail was hanging crooked and I had on a night gown and some sweatpants. I went to her kitchen table and laid out all of his credit cards and checkbooks from our company and our personal accounts that were also in my name on the table. I gave her the keys to his house and the truck. I told her I was tired of him beating on me and he promised that when he came back from out of town that he was gonna do it again and I started crying. She grabbed me and hugged me so tight. I said, "Momma why he don't love me?" She said, "Stop crying baby. It's gone be alright. He ain't got sense the first. I'm sick of his stanking ass."

She rarely cursed so I knew she was mad. "He just doesn't appreciate me. I can't do anything good enough that makes him happy. I don't know why he hates me so much and I do anything he tells me to do." "Baby it ain't you and it ain't your fault. He got some mental issues baby. You see something ain't right in his head. He just need to stop all that drinking and go get him some help before he end up in jail somewhere." "I really wanted my family to work Ms. Shaw but I just cant take it no more. I'm tired of being scared of him. You don't know the half of the things that he's done to me and I still stayed with him. But I cant do it no more. That's all his financial stuff and I didn't take any of his things out the house. I only got my clothes and shoes and the kids' clothes and shoes."

"I'm sorry baby but I understand. You got to do what you feel is best for you. He just a fool! I can't wait until his dumb butt get back. He gon be in for a rude awakening. Maybe this will let him know he needs to get his act together. You gon be okay baby? Where you gon go? You need some money?" I said, "I'm gon be ok no thank you. I'm going to my mom's house." She said, "Ok you know I love you Skye?" I said "I love you to momma and then I left."

I hadn't had time to explain what was going on to Soni. When I called her she didn't ask any questions she just did what I asked her to do for me. She always had my back. I don't care what, I know I can always depend on Soni. When I made it back to the car I told her everything that happened. She asked me why was this time any different than the others. She wasn't trying to be funny, she just wanted to know because I had never taken these drastic measures. I said I just woke up and something told me I had to leave now. So I did. It was really like I didn't have a choice. It was like I was being lead to go. She said "thank you Lord Jesus! That wasn't nothing but the Holy Spirit speaking to you and leading you out of harms way. I been told you, you have a discerning spirit and God reveals things to you but you just haven't tapped into your gift yet. I sho do wish He would talk to me like He talks to you.

Oh, thank you Jesus just for who you are! He said touch not my anointed and Skye you are anointed and Raheem is gonna pay for all the things he has done to you. Vengeance is mine said the Lord. No weapons formed against you shall prosper. I decree and declare in the name of Jesus! Yeah devil I know you mad! You thought you was gon get her by using another one of your demons and God still kept her! You couldn't have her years ago when you tried to kill her and you cant have her now!" She was quoting scriptures and speaking in tongues. I was just crying because I heard her and I believed everything she was professing. I silently thanked God as she was speaking. Once she calmed down she asked me what was I gonna do now? "Do you have a plan?" I said "not really but I think I just want to go get me a hotel room with a kitchen so I can feed my kids. We can't eat out everyday and I don't have a car now and I'm not ready to go into details with my mom."

So we rode around until we found something far enough away where Raheem would not find me because he was gonna look for me. I finally got my kids and some clothes and Soni dropped us off to get settled in our temporary home. I was glad that I had been smart enough not to spend every lil dime he gave to me, and it wasn't often that he gave me money like that. He would buy me anything but rarely put lump sums in my hand. So I did have a little piece of money but it wasn't gone last long so I had to come up with a plan and I had to do it fast. It was the weekend so I was glad I didn't have to worry about Nandi getting to school for the next few days. I had the most amazing sleep that night. I woke up and was a little confused about where I was. The kids were watching cartoons and eating cereal. Lil Raheem only had cereal in his bowl. If he would've had milk it was gonna look like a disaster in there. I stretched and smile because I felt good. I didn't feel like I had to do nothing special but lay in this big bed and be happy. After a while I got up to use the bathroom and when I came back out I fixed me some hot tea and grabbed my phone off the kitchen counter.

I had 32 missed calls from Raheem and 17 voice messages. As I listened to the first message he was cursing me out, "Bitch when I find you uma fuck you up."

"Ho bring me my son on the next." "Bitch you'll be back cause you ain't got nothing."

"Baby I'm sorry I love you. Call me so we can talk and you can come on back home man. Why you doing this to our family? The girls just got here and they asking for they brother and they sister. Man quit playing and come home before you make me mad."

"You so stupid, don't nobody want yo ass but me."

"Please come home."

"Fuck you bitch I can have any broad, stay yo broke ass where you at."

It went on and on. I just shook my head grabbed a donut and went and laid back down. He started calling back about 20 minutes later and I turned the ringer off cause I didn't want to hear anything he had to say. We lived in the hotel for almost a month.

I didn't take any of his calls and I didn't go anywhere I thought he might be. It would be around 3 months. Before I finally decided to speak with him. I needed a car so I had to ask him for money because I didn't have it. I'd found an apartment that allowed me to rent a three bedroom from them without having a job because I paid my rent up for 3 months in advance. I didn't have anything to put in it but it was the most peaceful time I had had in a long time. For months my kids and I slept on a pallet made from quilts and comforters my mom had given me. She had also given us lots of towels and wash cloths. I bought a 19 colored tv and a VCR from Walmart along with a cheap 8-piece pots and pans set. I got 4 spoons, 4 forks, 2 butter knives, 1 sharp butcher knife, paper plates, 3 bowls and 4 glasses. I also bought 3 Barney and Friends DVD's and 3 Elmo Sesame Street DVD's on sale for $5 each. I needed that so the kids wouldn't drive me crazy. I got in touch with Rod and told him I needed is help. He came through and brought me a washer and a dryer he had got form somebody he knew was selling it. He took me to the grocery store cause he had food stamps he bought from somebody.

All in all, things were coming together. I finally had Shanti to take me to meet Raheem at the bank so he could take my name off of the accounts because legally I still could go into a bank and fill out a withdrawal form and get money but I wasn't trying to create no drama. I signed the paperwork and he gave me $5000 dollars to get a car. This cheap ass negro! He had at least $300,000.00 collectively in those accounts. Not to mention the money he had in safe's at different locations. He was being petty but I said thank you and left. My friends were great at trying to keep me cheered up. We would still hang out together at each other's homes sometimes. But I did miss him, the good him. So I started back talking to him and going out with him but I wouldn't move back in the house cause I know during that three month break up he was wilding out there in them streets.

I really moved out to show him that I would leave him so he would start treating me right because I wanted him to feel the burn of my absence. So he basically moved in with me. We were back on again. He hadn't been mean to me. My birthday came around and he took me to the car lot and paid $16,000.00 cash for me a Lexus GS 300. I still didn't have a job so Shanti said her sister had a food stand next to her husbands strip club and I could work in there cooking and selling food if I needed to, and I needed to because Raheem wasn't about to help me pay rent on my apartment when we had a house we could go back too. It was a fun job. I met a lot of people and I made enough to pay my bills.

When Raheem found out I was working there he lost his mind. Told me I couldn't work there. But I didn't stop because I liked what I was doing and I was making my own money. Plus it wasn't like it was gonna be forever. I had been looking for jobs and had went on an interview with a juvenile detention center and had been offered the job, contingent upon my background check clearing. And human resource department said it would only take a week or so for that to clear, so I was happy about that. One night Shanti and I decided to go out and I parked my car across from the food stand and hopped in her Expedition with her. When I got back to my car the front windshield had been shattered with a big Hennessy bottle by a maniac….. Raheem of course. People were standing around outside as I was looking dumbfounded, but I already knew Raheem had done it.

YOU REAL SLICK THO

There were a couple of dudes standing outside and one of them spoke up and said, "a lil shawty I saw the whole thing." This big ass black gorilla looking dude went up to the car and pulled on the door handle of all the doors then he laid across the car like he was trying to see if it was warm, I'm guessing. I swea I thought he was Greg Street cause they was the same kinda ugly! Lol!! I was like damn V-103 gon have to come bail this dude out of jail! Then dude walked to his car and came back with a huge ass bottle of Hennessy. You know them big thick one's?" I said, "Yeah the bottle laying right here next to my car tire." "Man dude went crazy all of a sudden and just started banging the windshield with the bottle. I thought the bottle was gonna break but like I said that bitch was thick as hell bruh! Man he hit the window bout five times! "whop, whop, whop, whop, whop Lol! Then he dropped the bottle and just walked back to his car and drove off. We was cracking up the whole time saying damn somebody gon be mad as hell lol!" I didn't see shit funny and I guess he could tell by my facial expression because he stopped laughing and said, "nawl.... but real talk tho, that was some ho shit! Real niggas don't do crazy shit like that, chics do." Then they walked away. I drove around with my windshield messed up like that for two weeks. I didn't report it to my insurance company because the deductible was higher than it cost to order it from a glass company and let them install it so that's what I did.

I couldn't understand for the life of me why he would do that. I mean, word on the street was that he was dating a stripper chick they called Hunni. I didn't know cause I wasn't keeping tabs on him. I started my job with that broken window and a glass company came right out on the job site and replaced the windshield in about an hour or so. I was back in business. I liked my job enough. It wasn't hard at all. I liked taking to the kids about being respectful and honoring their parents even though a lot of the parents were on drugs and they had been in and out of foster care. Most all of them said they felt a certain type of way about their parents. So being respectful meant nothing to them.

I liked listening to their stories. I couldn't imagine living the lives that a lot of them had. Some of the girls had been pimped out and they were only 10 years old and up. Some of the boys had to be the man of the house, paying bills and taking care of their younger siblings and they were barely 16 years old. I felt so sorry for them because I couldn't relate to any of their circumstance. I wasn't raised around any of that and growing up none of my friends had been locked up in juvenile before. I had to learn to adjust to the demands of the job. I was a counselor, mother, teacher, confidant, and an inspirer. I never judged them. I viewed them as if they could be one of my children. You never know what paths your own children my have to cross. So I always treated them with respect because everyone deserved respect, even little babies that couldn't talk and speak up for them selves.

After that fiasco with my car window being broken I backed up from Raheem a lot more. I was loving my new found independence. I was slowly beginning to accept that this wasn't going to be my family and I was okay with that. The thing I missed the most concerning our lives together was Chayla and Shelby. I missed them so much. It's funny that when you separate yourself from a man you have to separate yourself from his kids and his family. If not and you still hanging at family functions then you are sending mixed messages. You might not believe it but it's true. I didn't plan on going to anymore of his family events cause I was done with this dude and everything attached to him. Yeah, so......go figure. I started back talking to him.

We were mostly at my apartment because I didn't want to stay at the house we had because I could speculate on what he was doing by what he's done in the past, and acknowledge that the heart doesn't lie. My heart and the streets, know what he's been doing. We would go stay at the house every now and again. He even gave me my key back that I'd given his mom. Everything seemed to be going great. We haven't had a fight in months. However, my feelings for him had begun to diminish daily. I just hated him sometimes. I couldn't understand why he didn't love me even though he swore up and down that he did. Even though things weren't as bad as they had been I felt like he had something else going on. Plus, I had asked him about the stripper and he said it wasn't true.

One day, bout a month later, I had been trying to reach him and he wasn't answering his phone. I rode over to the house and rang the doorbell. He didn't answer but I heard footsteps on those hardwood floors. I started beating on the door and still no answer. I walked around to the garage and I saw someone peeking out of the blinds in the upstairs bedroom that we once shared. I screamed "I know you in there stupid ass boy cause I can hear you walking around and I saw the blinds move"! Then instead of just lifting the garage door up, I turned the handle and it locked it. I was heated about that cause I could've gotten in the house that way. Then I picked up a rock and threw it at the bedroom window and it broke. I was like oh shit!

He gon kill me for that. It was too late then. I started to throw more rocks and busted out more windows. All the while I was saying I know you're in there and I ain't going nowhere until you come out. You must have a bitch in there? I had walked all the way around the house trying to get in but there was no use. It was like Fort Knox around there. I went and sat on my car for about 20 minutes just talking trash about how I wasn't going nowhere. Then I remembered that I had a big stick about 3 feet long with and iron tip on it I kept my trunk. It was a lovely gift my mom had given me to bust a bitch in the head in case they tried me. I got the stick out my trunk and was walking back and forth in front of the garage threatened to bust the sliding glass door in the back of the house if he didn't open the door. I heard a car pulling into the driveway and It was Raheem and his homeboy Shot Caller in his truck.

If you could've seen the look on my face at that moment! I'm thinking, how in the hell is he not in the house. I know I heard somebody in that damn house! He is gon kill me for breaking his windows! He got out the car and walked toward me. I took a stance holding my stick. He said "what's up?" I said, "Nothing who's in the house?" He saw glass on the ground and said, "You don lost your mind? What the hell you break my windows for?" I said,"How you know I was over here? I called your phone bout 20 times and you never answered." "Girl you broke this window too?" he said like he didn't hear my question. He started walking towards me and I took a step back and said, "You might beat my ass today but I'm gon get at least one good lick in upside your head with this stick."

He stopped in his tracks and just shook his head and said I was tripping. "Open the door Raheem." He patted his pockets and said, "I think I left them in the truck." He walked back like he was looking for them in there too. Then he said, "I must've left them at my momma's house." I said, "yeah?" Then I called his mom and asked did Raheem leave his keys over there? She said "When? I haven't seen that boy all day and I couldn't have missed him cause I ain't been nowhere." I said, "Okay he probably left them in the house." She said "Is he with you?" I said, "Yeah he's right here." "She asked how did he lock himself out the door? "He's retarded but thanks ma."

I hung up. "So your momma ain't seen you all day, but you left your keys at her house? Well we need to call the police cause somebody is in your house." He started saying, "You so stupid ain't nobody in there and you gon pay for those windows." "I ain't paying for nothing! You think you so slick. I don't know how you did it but I know you was in that house." I got in my car and drove off feeling defeated. I knew he was in there but I couldn't prove it. He didn't touch me for breaking the windows and that proved to me in itself that he was guilty.

Any other time I would've been swollen up behind breaking his windows. It wasn't until months later that I learned that he had been there the whole time. He had snuck out the house through the basement door while I was making threats and called Shot Caller to come pick him up from the next street over. Time passed and he was more and more distant. I knew he was still cheating. I needed to get away and just clear my mind but not without my kids. I told him that I was booking a weekend trip to Lake Lanier with the kids and he could come if he wanted too. He declined to go and that was cool with me. After I had all four of the kids' bags packed for the weekend and we were all most at the interstate he called my phone and said he wanted to go. I told him where I was and he had on of his partners to drop him off to us.

I was enjoying myself playing with the kids. We played all kinds of games like hide and seek, jumped up and down on the beds, ate a lot of great junk food and just hung out at the pool the majority of the time. I could see him over at the bar on his phone. I know he was talking to her. Later that night after the kids were asleep we were sitting on the floor talking and he was telling me how much he loved me and he couldn't see himself with anybody else. "I know I've done some things that hurt you Skye and I'm truly sorry. I want my family back. I don't want to live in separate households. We belong together in the same house."

"Well, that must mean we about to get another house cause I can't live there anymore. You have had too many girls over there and I don't feel like that's my home anymore." "Baby I'll buy us another house. Whatever it takes, I'll do it. I just know we all can't live comfortably in your 3-bedroom apartment." "Ok let's do it. I just need you to be honest with me. If you don't want us anymore, then just say that. I don't want to share my man with anyone. If being with someone else makes you happy then that's where you should be. And although it may hurt me to my core, at the end of the day I want you to be happy, and I want to be happy too." He kept saying "It's all about you baby. I'm gonna do better I promise." "Yeah Raheem you said that before and nothing has changed. I'm good to you and you don't appreciate it. Just go on and live your life, make you happy. Because if you messing with the stripper and you're confused about which one you should choose to be with, allow me help you out with that, choose her. Cause evidently that's where you really want to be. And you don't have not one more time to put your hands on me. You have daughters. How would you feel if a dude did to them the things that you've done to me? I swea if you don't get it together and show me that this is what you want then I'm leaving you Raheem, for real, not still messing around with you from time to time. I'm not gone fuck with you." "Noooo I really want to be with you Skye. I'm not gonna mess with her no more." "Who were you on the phone with earlier today at the bar?" "I was talking to Tela." "Well it appears that Tela had you looking all goofy eyed. He must've been saying something good and that's some gay ass shit for you to be blushing on the phone with another man.

Anyway what I'm trying to let you know is it's ok for us not to be together. Things happen, people change their minds all the time about what the thought they wanted." "Like I said Skye from now on it's just you and me. I don't want nobody else but you." I wanted to believe him but I didn't. The weekend was over and it was time to get back to reality. Once we got back to Atlanta we went to his mom's house because I had to braid Shelby's hair before she went back home. Raheem had said that Chayla's mom had told him that she didn't want me combing her daughter's hair. And he was cool with it until we were going out somewhere and all the girls had their hair done but Chayla.

Anyway we were at his mom's house and he said he was gonna go horse back riding with McDeel. I said "It's 7:30pm. Where ya'll riding at in he dark?" "We just gon go riding." I said ok. So needless to say, he didn't come home that night. I prayed and asked God to reveal the things I need to see regarding him. I know it might hurt Lord but I need to see for myself what he's doing. So I got up extra early the next morning and got dressed for work. I got the kids up so I could take them to my mom's house to go to school. I went to his house and opened the door with my key. I deactivated the alarm and called out his name to alert him as I started up the stairs because I knew he kept his gun on the nightstand.

When I got to the bedroom door I tried to turn the knob and it was locked. I said, "Raheem open the door!" I heard movement on the other side of the door and as I leaned in to hear better I heard him mumbling "shit! Man why she come over here? Damn! Aye man….throw me some shorts." I immediately started trying to kick in the door. Boom! Boom! Boom! "You got a girl in there? I can't believe you got a girl in there!" Boom! Boom! I kick again. "But you suppose to been back at the house when you finished riding horses?"

"A man throw me some shorts." "Throw you some shorts? You mean to tell me you in here laid up with another chic after we just got back last night from a family vacation! You fucking another girl when less than a couple hours ago you was eating out every hole I got? Open the door lame ass nigga! So, this what you were doing on the phone at the pool, making arrangements to get with this broad? You ain't shit!" In the midst of me talking he rushed out the door and grabbed me.

We stumbled down the stairs and I was trying my best to knock his head off. He grabbed me by may wrist and put them behind my back and held me tightly. I wanted to scream! I calmly said "Turn me a loose. You smell just like her. You got dried up coochie juice on your face. You nasty bastard! You was just sucking on my yoni and had your tongue up in my butt last night but I guess that wasn't enough. Turn me loose!"

"I ain't gone let you go until you calm down."

"I'm calm!"

"You gon try to fight that girl?"

"Really? When have you ever known me to be out here fighting? I'm dressed for work and that's where I'm going as soon as I leave here."

"Ok I'm gon turn you loose." When he let me go I said with your stanking face ass. I sat down on the sofa and he sat in the chair across from me.

"I just ain't gon never be enough for you huh? You beat on me for breathing. You embarrass me in front of anybody for no reason. Nothing I do is good enough for you. So who is the girl upstairs? Is this the same stripper chic they called Hunni that I asked you about and you said you didn't mess with her?" He said , "Yeah but that's not her name."

"Fuck what her name is, tell her to come downstairs." "Why?" Raheem asked.

"I just want to see who you just destroyed our family for."

"Man if I tell her to come down here you gon be trying to fight."

"Look at me. I'm dressed for work and as soon as I leave here that's where I'm going.

I ain't got time to be fighting her."

"Hey girl, come downstairs." Raheem commanded.

"Oh, so it's hey girl now? So you don't know her name?"

She came downstairs wearing his orange polo tee shirt and a pair of jeans. She was high yella with a long ponytail that hung to her butt and had red lipstick smeared on her face. She looked like she had had an interesting night. I asked her, her name. She said, "Harrlot with two R's".

I said, "Harlot? Lol! Do you even know what that means? That's the name given to 16th century whores! Your momma named you that? Oh that's your stripper name?"

"Yeah that's my dance name but my real name is Jontiel." She replied.

"Stripper, dancer same thing alike. Okay so anyway what did he tell you about us, and our relationship? Who does he say I am?"

"He just said you won't leave him alone. He made you leave and you still be bothering him." Lol!!!

I busted out laughing. "So I'm the disillusioned baby momma that won't t let go? And you probably really believe him." I turned and looked at Raheem and said,

"You know damn well I ain't trying to make you be with me. I left you remember? Then gave you another chance to redeem yourself and prove to me that you want this relationship. Just last night I was telling you you're gonna have to buy another house because I wasn't staying where you've brought God knows how many women over here since I left. Raheem didn't you just say you wanted your family back? All that begging and promising you was doing. For what? You know damn well that ain't what you want. And for the first time since I've been in this relationship with you, I'm ready to accept that. I am dying laughing on the inside just thinking about all the times you've called me every bitch and ho in the book. You had the unmitigated gall to tell me I wasn't shit and that nobody was gonna want me. But you end up with this bitch that will buss it wide open in front ya homeboys, ya homegirls, ya daddy and ya momma if they got a dollar. She don't give a damn. What the hell she care? She bout her money, it don't matter who gives it to her. That's ya bitch and ya ho right there. Lol! Girl let me enlightened you on something. This nigga will tell you anything you want to hear to get what he wants from you. I know he's charming and he doesn't mind spending his money on you, that's cause he a trick. Well, I guess it ain't tricking if you got it. He loves to have a good time. When he's doing all that it can't help but to grab your attention. So it could've been hard for you to tell he had a woman with all the balling ya'll doing. But nah let me stop playing, I can't give you that much credit, you just didn't care.

You knew about me. Ain't no way in hell you didn't. You know when a dude has a girl no matter how many times he tells you he doesn't. A woman's intuition never fails her. We're born with it. It's that feeling you get in your gut that says, "something ain't right." It may be off a little bit on all the particulars but at the end of the day she always ends up being right. You were in the house with him that day I busted out all his windows, all quiet and shit. Because, that's what side bitches do. They know to shut the fuck up. I guess the perks that come with having to shut the fuck up, out weigh the how would I feel if it were me factor. Now you're about to reap all the benefits that come along with being with him. This nigga lie just cause he got a mouth.

He telling you I won't leave him alone. Lying to you cause this man has been living with me in my apartment. The only time we come here is when we have all the kids together so they can have enough room to run around and play with their toys that are here. So Harrlot? Jontiel or whatever your name is you don't ever have to worry about me coming over here interrupting y'all moment or disturbing y'all ecstasy. You just did me a big favor and I thank you for that. You can have him. You can tell your friends you took him from me, baby it don't even matter. I don't want him. You just freed me from a place I did not know how to escape from. I'm forever indebted to you! But I'm gonna tell you this tho, this nigga gon beat yo ass black and blue and you super light skinned too. Umm ummm umm, baby you can get ready cause it's coming. Not because of anything that you did, but because I'm not gonna fuck with him and he's gon blame you for it. You're about to wear some of the worst ass whippings you can't hardly begin to imagine. Whew, good Lord! Now I ain't got to worry about you harassing me. You have done everything to embarrass me."

NEGROS AIN'T SHYT

"You've humiliated me in front of my friends and beat me for the last time. This was the ultimate disrespect. You never deserved me anyway. Don't no real man want his lady walking around beat up with black eyes. You have two daughters that are going to grow up into beautiful young ladies. How would you feel if one of their boyfriends beat on them like you've always beaten on me? Every little girl wants a man like their daddy, I pray God never grants them that disadvantage. Hear me when I say this. I don't want yo ass no more so stay the fuck away from me before I kill you. Did I make myself clear? Here are your keys and you don't have to worry about giving me mine back because they'll be changed just as soon as I make the phone call. Thank you again Harrlot. Y'all can carry on."

I smiled and turned to walk out the house and he came behind me and said, "Call me when you get off work baby with a smirk."

I turned around and spit in his face, which is the nastiest thing you can do to anyone. Then I walked to my car, got in and drove off….in a daze. I couldn't process what had just happened. I got to work and I knew I was there but I felt like a robot, just operating. My mind kept was replaying what had happened. I started having thoughts about what I should've said. I thought about how I should've been going upside his head and hers. My chest was burning so bad from the hurt that I was unconsciously rubbing it. Somehow I handled the situation with grace and class in their faces. All the while I was crying on the inside, but like a boss. I wouldn't give them the satisfaction of seeing my tears. The next couple of weeks came and went in a daze. I lost 12lbs in two weeks.

Every day, everything I did was routine. Wake up, cry. Get ready for work. Get the kids to school. Go to work. Get off work. Get the kids. Feed the kids. Check Nandi's homework. Give them a bath. Take a shower. Cry while in the shower so my kids don't hear me. Drink a glass of wine to settle my nerves. Lay in the bed with my kids watching tv until we fell asleep. Then I get back up and do the same thing the next day. I didn't want to talk to anybody so I stopped answering my phone. I didn't completely understand everything I was feeling. I kept wondering why he didn't love me.

Maybe I wasn't pretty or fine enough. It's like I wanted him but I didn't want him. I think I only felt that way because we had been together for so long and my life was all about us. I wanted him to hurt. I wanted him to feel the pain of loosing me. But he didn't. He kept on living his life and having fun while I was an emotional wreck. He came by my apartment about 3 weeks after we had officially broken up. He had been drinking and he was telling me that he loved me and he never meant to hurt me. As we sat outside on the steps just talking I said to him "if you leave her alone and stop messing with her I'll forget about everything that happened. We can get another house and move forward with our family." His response is one that is etched in my memory forever. He said I can't stop messing with her because she was what every man wanted. Every dude that looks at her wants her, and she wanted him so he couldn't stop messing with her." His words felt like hot lava pouring over me.

Hold up! Did this nigga just say what I thought he said? Cause all I heard was he couldn't stop messing with her. How could the man that I've tried so hard to love all these years tell me something like that with a straight face? After all the shit he put me through! Now I wasn't good enough? I sat there in disbelief and in silence for about 5 minutes. Then I told him okay. I got up off the steps and went in the house. I closed the door and locked it. Then I walk to my bedroom, laid on the bed and cried until I knew I was almost blind. Just when I thought I was all cried out a fresh set of tears would start. I mean I cried for the old and the new, the borrowed and the blue honey! I didn't think the human body had that much water in it!

Throughout all the things that I'd endured and allowed while being with him, this I felt by far was the hardest to accept. Rejection is a hard pill to swallow. I somehow found the energy to get up and get my life back. A life that was foreign to me but I had to live in what was now cause what it was didn't exist anymore. I had come to grips with what happened and I no longer wanted to be with someone that didn't want to be with me. I started to breathe again. Raheem called not long after that incident and said he wanted to come get his son so he could spend the night with him. I said, "I don't know your girlfriend enough to feel comfortable with her taking care of my child." He said, "I better get use to it cause that was who he was with and when his son was with him he was gonna be around her too."

I wanted to argue my point that this is the same chick I caught him with, but I knew it wouldn't do any good. I knew I didn't want to ever be with him again and if I kept his son away from him, he was gonna feel like I was doing it to get back at him. So

I knew the only way to prove him wrong was to let my son go with him, even though I didn't want my baby to go. He was only 2 years old and I was so attached to him and really protective of my kids. I told him he could pick him up from my mom's house at around 4:00 that afternoon and I hung up the phone. I knew that he wasn't expecting me to say that. A few weeks went by and I was starting feel better but I would still have my days when I would struggle with what was going on in my head and my heart. I got off work about an hour early today so I went to my mom's house to pick up my kids. The only thing on my mind was getting home and getting in my bed because I felt so drained.

When I walked in the door I guess my mom could see the look of despair on my face and she said, "Why don't you just go on home and get some rest? The kids can stay with me tonight." I asked her if she was sure? She said "yeah, you look like you need a break." So I went into the kitchen where Nandi was coloring and eating grapes. She looked up and said, "Hey momma look what I did!"

"Oooow that's so pretty baby." "I colored it for you momma. It's a rainbow."

"I love it punkin, thank you. Grand momma said she wanted you and your brother to spend the night with her. Do you want to stay?"

"Yeah cause grandma ain't gonna make me go to school and I can sleep a long time." I laughed and said, "You're going to school shawty. You must've forgot about the field trip to Fernbank Museum?"

"Ohhh yeah, I gotta go to school tomorrow cause I'm the class monitor and somebody gotta watch out for them bad children in my class."

I started laughing and said, "You kill me, how come everybody bad but you?" She just smiled her beautiful smile, hunched up her shoulders, and said, "I can't help it if I'm good, momma." I hugged her and kissed her on the lips. "I love you lil girl. Let me go upstairs and see what your lil brother doing." "Ooooh momma you need to take that bad lil boy with you. He threw his pacifier at grand momma and it almost hit her in the face!

All because she wouldn't move out from in front the tv when he was watching Elmo on Sesame Street. That's a bad lil baby! He better be gladdd it wasn't me cause I woulda beat him!" "Girl hush, you was just like that about Barney so stop playing". I went to my mom's room and lil Raheem was sitting in the middle of the bed with a pacifier in his mouth and one in each hand. I snuck up on him and said "boo!" He didn't even flinch. He looked up at me and said,"Shut up ugly momma." I grabbed him, tickled him and said, "Who you telling to shut up boy?" He was laughing and slobbering with that pacifier still in his mouth.

He had to have his paci. I kept at least 5 because if he got mad at you he would take it out his mouth and throw it at you, but when he couldn't find it he would cry like hell. I stayed and played with him and Nandi for almost 2 hours before they were telling me bye. I welcomed the me time even though I knew I was gonna spend it crying. When I got home and took a hot bubble bath and sipped on a glass of wine while teardrops fell from my eyes, slid down my face and into the now luke warm water. I was still healing from my heartbreak, but I knew I was gonna be alright. The phone had been ringing while I was in the tub and I didn't care. Whoever it was had to wait until I was done. I didn't feel like talking anyway. I hoped it wasn't my mom telling me to come get my son because he wouldn't stop crying. I wasn't going back to get him for nothing. She was stuck with him.

When I got out and dried off and rubbed some chocolate soufflé body butter on. I smelled just like a Hershey bar. I put on a tee shirt and some panties then I picked up the phone to see if I had any voice messages. I didn't but I had 3 missed calls from Raheem. Really? Why was he calling me? Anyway, I wasn't about to call him back. I felt the wine settling my nerves and I knew I needed to eat something because my stomach was growling but I wasn't hungry but I ate a few graham crackers and poured myself another glass of wine, got in the bed, turned on the tv and let it watch me because I was out like a light. I dreamed a dream that I was all too familiar with, I was teaching the kids in my neighborhood how to fly again. I remember researching what this dream of flying meant, the answers I got was that dreaming of flying embody freedom, freedom from a situation, relationship, belief, or attitude. Often flying dreams occur after you have moved on from something. Or they may occur when you need to leave a situation. Sometimes these dreams can be about fear or a lack of freedom.

I was awakened from this flying dream by the incessant ringing of my phone. "Hello?" "Where my baby at?" "He's at my mom's house." "Aight." Then he hung up the phone. So I hung up the phone and went back to sleep. Ten minutes later my phone was ringing again just as I was dozing back off. "HELLO!" "Where Nandi at?" "Her and the baby are at my mom's. Why?" He hung up the phone. I thought it was weird that he kept calling asking the same questions but I just shook it off that he was a special kind of stupid. The phone rung again and I picked it up and said "stop calling me I gotta go to work in the morning!" He said, "you said they're at your moms house?" I said "yeah" and hung up the phone again. This time I sat up in the bed and said to myself, why does he keep calling me? Before I could complete that thought all I heard was this big loud noise. Bam! Bam! Bam! He was kicking by front door in. I had this big green couch pushed up to the door because I always felt like I needed to keep myself safe so that was my attempt at a barrier.

My heart immediately started beating fast cause I knew it was Raheem. I called 911.

"911 what's your emergency?"

"Please send the police! My ex boyfriend is kicking in my door."

"What's his name, ma'am?"

"Raheem Shaw. Please hurry up!! I know he's gonna kill me."

"Just stay on the phone ma'am I've already dispatched 3 units to your location."

Bam! Bam! Bam!. "Oh my God please!!! Hurry up!"

"I'm here with you ma'am just stay on the phone."

"He just got through the door!" Raheem had managed to kick the door open enough to squeeze in and push the large sofa back. He started walking toward me and I told the operator he was going to kill me. I was still sitting on the bed with the covers across my legs when he walked into my room and asked, "Who you talking to?"

I said "my mom" because I didn't want him to know it was the police.

"Keep him talking ma'am."

"What are you telling your mom?" Raheem asked.

"I'm telling her how you just kicked in my door for

nothing and I don't even know why you're over here anyway, we don't go together anymore."

"Well tell your mom you're on my time now." He snatched the phone out of my hand, ripped it out of the wall and slapped me across the face with it.

I fell back on the bed from the blow of the hit. He sat on top of me and brutally pummeled me in my face. The punches were coming so rapid and forcefully that I could hardly form a thought as to why this was happening? I couldn't catch my breath. I couldn't remember a time when I'd ever been hit that hard. He got up and pulled me out of the bed by my hair and slung me around like a rag doll. I could hear the braids in my hair being ripped out. Everything was happening so fast that I felt like I was having an out of body experience. He started punching me again in my face and my stomach. I doubled over from the pain. In my head I was saying why are you doing this but I couldn't get a word out my mouth.

I don't even remember screaming because I couldn't find my voice.

"Bitch I'm gonna kill you."

He threw me into the wall and I slid down. I thought I was gonna be able to say please stop but I couldn't because he snatched me up off the floor and punched me in my mouth and I saw blood splatter across the wall. He threw me on the floor and climbed on top of me and said again,

"Bitch I'm gonna kill you".

I believed him.

He placed his hands around my neck and pressed his thumbs in my throat. I couldn't breathe. I wondered where was the police? My eyes felt like they were popping out of their sockets. He kept saying he was going to kill me. I felt like I was blacking out and I remember thinking I didn't want to die like this. I thought about yesterday was the last day I would ever see my children. In my mind I said God please save me.

Almost instantly he turned my neck a loose and I caught my breath and said, "My babies!" He got up off of me and walked out of the room. I laid on the floor a few seconds gasping for air. I sat up and that's when I heard the house alarm blaring. I crawled to the bedroom door. I couldn't see out of my right eye at all and barely out of my left. I knew I had to get away from him because if I didn't he was going to complete the mission he was on to kill me. I could see he was trying to close the door but because he had kicked the whole frame off, it wouldn't close. When he finally found out he couldn't close it he started trying to disarm the alarm but he didn't have the new code.

By now I had gotten up off the floor and started to feel my way down the hall slowly holding onto the wall. He didn't notice me with all the noise coming from the alarm. I made it to the living room and saw the patio door and prayed that it wasn't locked. I got to the door turned the knob opened it and locked it back before I left out. I looked down at the ground and said how am I going to jump from this two story balcony? I crawled over the wrought iron bannister and started trying to shimmy down the bars and the devil came out on the porch reached over and grabbed my arms trying to pull me back up. I realized that it was hard for him to pull me up and he was struggling so I turned the bars a loose. My wrist slipped through his hands and fell two stories onto the downstairs neighbors patio. I landed straddled on the iron railed bar.

At that time, I didn't feel a thing. I then fell inside on their porch, jumped up and started beating on her door and windows screaming for help saying, "He's trying to kill me!"

Nobody was home. I saw him jump down off my patio and the only thing I said as he was descending is God please let him break his leg! He didn't. I was shocked. He walked over toward me and I was wondering where in the hell was the police? I backed as far back into the corner of her porch as I could. He couldn't reach me because the foundation was about a foot high from the ground. He finally stepped up reached over and caught me by my hair and pulled me towards him.

The bannister reached me at my chest. I wrapped my arms through the bars and held on tightly because he was now trying to pull me over it. The fear I had was so overwhelming that I lost control of my bladder and peed myself. I got nervous because I been told growing up if you loose your bladder or your bowels if you go shot or something that it meant you were going to die. The blows were steady coming to my face and head and I had no more fight in me so I let go of the bars and he jerked me over the rail scraping the skin off my legs. He threw me on the ground and I heard the voice of my neighbor from upstairs saying, "Don't you touch her no more dammit! I done called the police on your ass so don't put your hands on her again." He then picked me up off the ground and started walking towards his car and she said, "Put her down you bastard!"

He dropped me on the ground, kicked me and walked away. I scrambled to my feet as fast as I could, running pass her trying to make my way up the stairs that lead to her front door, bypassing my own apartment. I went into her apartment and closed the door behind me. She was pushing on the door as I was attempting to lock it. She came in and said, "It's me baby. She locked the door and when she turned and looked at me she gasped and put her hand up to her mouth with a look on her face I assume was horror."

At the moment I couldn't focus on what had her standing there as if she was frozen in time because I was frantically searching for her telephone. I spotted it on the wall in the kitchen and grabbed it to dial 911. She said she had already called 911 but I had started speaking to the operator.

"911 what's your emergency?"

"He's trying to kill me! Please send the police, please help me!"

“Ma'am they are on the way. Is he still there?”

“No he left.”

"Are you in a safe place?”

“I'm at my next-door neighbor's house.

Please send the police ma'am he might still be outside!” She kept trying to reassure me and seconds later there was a knock at the door saying this is the Clayton County police open the door. I told her thank you and hung up the phone.

My neighbor opened her door and at least nine police officers entered her apartment. One of the officers identified himself as Sgt. Gates. “You're safe now, we're here to help.” He asked “do you know who did this to you?”

I didn't know I was in shock, but I was shaking violently and my teeth were chattering. The sergeant asked my neighbor for a blanket. I answered, “Raheem Shaw.” I gave them his address, his momma's address, his telephone number, height, weight, and social security number! I don't know where all this information was coming from but it was flowing out like a running faucet. There was another officer standing nearby writing everything down that I said. There were at least nine or ten officers in that apartment. They were all looking at me and listening to what I said. A few of them were pacing back and forth. I couldn't gage their emotions but I could see the look of disgust on their faces, like if they could get their hands on him, the things they would do to him. Not long after Sgt. Gates had questions the paramedics entered.

They strapped me down on a gurney and started out the door and down the stairs. All I kept hearing was the repeated police radio traffic, “Dispatch unit 22?” “Go for unit 22.” “10-25, 10-15?” “10-74 possible 273D, 217, 240 and a 242 copy?” “10-4 what's the 10-45 on the victim?” “That's a 10-45B, 10-45C copy?” “10-4, 10-26.” When I arrived at the hospital one of the nurses asked me if there was a next of kin she could call to let them know where I was. I knew I didn't want to call my mom so I gave her Shanti's number. She said she was going to call her and said that the doctor would be with me shortly. My mind was in a fog. I really didn't believe that this had just happened. I was replaying the whole incident, and as I searched his face, all I could see was rage in his eyes, and I kept hearing him say he was going to kill me.

LIVING IN FEAR

Lost in my thoughts I didn't hear the x-ray tech come in until he said "Ms. Patterson my name is Shelton, I'm going to take you to have some x-rays done. The doctor ordered them just to be sure you don't have any internal injuries that he can't see just by looking at you.

Are you okay with that?"

I said yes. "Are you pregnant?" No.

"Have you had any surgeries in the last twelve months?"
"No."

"Okay well let's get you down to x-ray."

I didn't say anything as he rolled me out of the room and down the hall. I was lost in my thoughts again. This time I cringed and gritted my teeth at the memory of how hard and rapid the blows where connecting to my face. I don't ever remember him hitting me that hard.

After I returned from x-ray Shanti was sitting in a chair in my room while her boyfriend Tela was standing in the corner with his arms folded across his chest. She gasped when she finally got a clear view of my face. I immediately asked for a mirror. The nurse from earlier was also there and she responded that I couldn't have the mirror just yet. Shanti said "you're still pretty as ever" but I didn't believe her because Tela was shaking his head and pacing back and forth. I asked again for a mirror and Shanti said "no!" I just decided to drop it for now. A little while later KK and Shot Caller walked in. I heard KK saying "man he didn't have to do that girl like that." I knew I looked a mess at that very moment and there was no use in looking in a mirror for evidence of what I already knew existed. I ended up staying there a couple more hours for observation. I was discharged with a couple of prescriptions for pain and a referral to follow up with a Cranial Specialist. We got in the car getting ready to pull off when Shot Caller walked over to the car with his cell phone extended to me saying that Raheem wanted to talk to me.

I couldn't believe the nerve of him to think that I wanted to speak to him. I told Shot Caller that he didn't have anything to say to me and he needed to be worried about what he was going to say to the police and I told Shanti to pull off. I asked her if it was okay if I stayed by her house because I couldn't go home and I didn't want to go to my mom's house. She said "of course." I pulled down the sun visor so I could look at my face but I couldn't' really see it clearly so I closed it back. I called my supervisor and told her that I wouldn't be coming to work the next day and asked if I could park my car at her house for a few days. She didn't ask any questions she simply said yes. We went by my apartment and I grabbed a few things and left. My supervisor lived close to me so the drive wasn't that far but that wasn't the issue, driving was.

I couldn't see very well because my left eye was swollen shut and the right eye was rapidly catching up. We pulled up and she opened the door to get the keys. She shook her head when she saw my face, took the keys from my hand and closed her door back. I don't know if she felt pity or disgust. I just couldn't beat myself up about it anymore than I already was. I got in the car with Shanti and called my mom as we were headed to her house. "Hey mom I need you to keep the kids a few days for me. Raheem jumped on me. I'm banged up pretty bad and I don't want my kids to see me looking like this. I'm gonna be alright. I'm in a safe place. I'll call you in a few days. I love you." I hung up the phone before she could start asking me questions I didn't have the strength to answer. We stopped to get my prescriptions filled then went to Shanti's house. All I wanted to do was take some pain medicine and go sleep. My head was pounding, and my face was throbbing! I took the medicine and got in the shower.

Once I dried off I had a chance to see myself in the mirror for the first time clearly and I couldn't believe what I saw. There was no way in the world I was ever gonna look the same again. I look just like the boy in the movie The Mask that Cher played in. I couldn't do anything but cry. Why would he do me like this? What had I done to deserve this? So many questions were floating around in my aching head. Somehow the medicine kicked in and the drowsiness started to wrap around me like a warm blanket and I slipped on a t shirt and some panties, got under the covers with hot tears rolling down my cheeks as I drifted off to sleep. I awoke the next morning in a sweat and I could barely catch my breath. Someone was trying to kill me and I was running for my life!

When I finally realized where I was I calmed down and my breathing returned back normal. It wasn't until I tried to get out the bed to go use the restroom that I truly remembered what had happened. My entire body was sore. It felt like I had bee hit by an 18 wheeler truck! I was limping because my right leg was bruised up bad from jumping off that balcony. I looked in the mirror when I washed my hands and my eyes where purple and black and my face had swollen up triple what it was before I went to sleep. I was so ugly! I just crawled back into bed, started crying and drifted back off to sleep. Later when I got up and got dressed we went down to Victim's Witness where I filled out a temporary restraining order and the process started so Raheem could be arrested.

They took pictures of my whole body and recorded a written and a verbal statement of what happened to me. We then went home and I took more pain medicine and fell asleep. It seemed as if the nightmares were never going to end. Every time I closed my eyes the same scenario played in my mind over and over again. It made me think if there was anything I could've done differently to prevent what happened and the answer was always the same…there was nothing I could have done that would've made the situation better, maybe worse but not better. I missed my children but I didn't have the strength or the explanation for what had happened to mommy so I'd have to settle for talking to them on the phone.

Two weeks passed and I was feeling a lot better and stronger. I had to face my family and my fears. The fear of what my kids were gonna say about what happened to me. No amount of makeup would cover the bruises to my face so I dare not try to hide them. I had to face the music. Once everyone got over the initial shock of seeing me and asking their questions of course they went into true Thomasville gangster we bout that life mode and was making plans on how they were gonna fuck Raheem up for what he had done to me. I heard everything they were saying and in my heart I agreed with them…he did need to be seen about but there was an undeniable fear that gripped me and I didn't want my people getting in trouble for trying to seek vengeance for me. So I spoke up and said, "I love ya'll but please just allow the police to handle it."

They weren't happy about it but they agreed to let it go for now. I wanted to go home with my kids and so I did just that. It didn't last for long because I couldn't sleep at night. Every sound or noise I heard made me wake up and look out of the window. I went behind myself and checked the locks on the door three or four times to make sure I had locked them. It became too overwhelming and I had to move. I broke my lease and for the first time in my adult life of being out on my own I had to move back in with my mom where I had the presence of others and I felt safe. I learned that Raheem had been arrested and in knowing that for the first time since the assault I finally had a night of sleep that was peaceful and sound because I knew he couldn't get close to me if he was locked up. For four months I could breathe again.

I flew out to Colorado where I had family because I needed a break for a few days. It was a much needed sabbatical and I thoroughly enjoyed the get away. I came home and got an apartment with Shanti and Taren. It was a nice place but I never really stayed there I still felt the need to be surrounded by my family. I eventually went back to work and things started feeling normal again. Of course the bruises hadn't healed completely and I had a couple of nosey people asking what happened to me but I just avoided their inquisitions by saying I'd rather not talk about it. Things seemed to be getting a little bit easier to bear day by day or so I thought. I never slept soundly at night because

I always heard every squeak or creak that the house held. That proved to be a good thing because one night I heard noises coming from one of the bedrooms across from mine.

Turned out it was Raheem trying to break in through the window in my nieces' room. Luckily the headboard on the bed was pushed up against the window and it stopped him from getting in. Another time I heard noises outside around the living room window and it was Raheem again trying to break into the house. I was always on edge. I made sure I checked my surroundings wherever I went. I never left or arrived anywhere without someone watching me exit out or enter my car. I was free and I was a prisoner at the same time. I got off work one day and my mom said that Raheem had come to get the baby for a while. I said ok and I walked up the sidewalk to talk with an old family friend. We were talking about life and how precious it was, how important family was and how I had the biggest crush on her nephew who would later in life be the father of my third child. It was sometime later while we were sitting in her den when I saw Raheem's car come down the street. I stayed a while longer so he would be gone when I got back. About 20 minutes passed and went back home only to find Raheem and my baby coming in the door and the baby had my set of keys in his hands. I asked him, "How did he get my keys." He said, "I left back out to go get him pampers and I didn't notice he had the keys until we got back here." He left and I told my mom she needed to get her locks changed because I knew how slick he was and I knew he had gotten a key made.

She said "he ain't that stupid" and I said, "But he is." I called Third World, which was the local music store in the hood that also made keys to ask Ashley, one of the girls who worked there if Raheem had been in there and if he'd gotten a key made she said that she had just gotten in but he was leaving as she was coming in and he had our baby with him. I knew then that he'd gotten a key made even if my mom dismissed it. I knew what I was dealing with. He was the spawn of Lucifer. My intuition was never wrong. True to life a few weeks later around 4am I woke up to the feeling of a presence standing over me. It was Raheem. I was scared to death, but I couldn't show it. I asked him what was he doing in my mom's house and how did he get in. He said he was magic. I told him he knew he wasn't suppose to be over there because he knew there was a restraining order against him. He said he had to see me and he wanted to taste me.

He started pulling back the covers and I said, "What are you doing? My son is asleep right next to me."

He said, "He's sleep and I wanna taste you."

"Please don't do this, just leave so you won't get in trouble for being over here."

He pulled the covers back and ripped my panties off. I was terrified. I wanted to scream but I didn't know if he had a weapon on him. I said I needed to use the bathroom. He told me to get up and he wrapped his hand up in my shirt and said, "Come on."

We got to the bathroom and I used it. Leaving out the bathroom all kinds of thoughts were going through my head….how can I get away? I could always scream but what if nobody heard me? I tried to think quick and said I wanted some water and headed toward the stairs and he jerked my shirt that he still had wrapped around his hands.

"Stop playing with me because all I have to do is knock yo ass out and carry you out the door." Raheem reminded me.

I knew he would do it so I stopped trying to think about getting away and started thinking bout staying alive. He pushed me back in the room and closed and locked the door while still holding my shirt in his hands. He then made me lay on the bed and he started kissing and licking me between my legs. I wanted to throw up! Then he said he had to be inside me. I told him please don't do that. You know you've been out there doing your thing and I really want you to just stop and leave.

He said, "Do you have any condoms?" As if I was

gonna say yes. I didn't have any because I wasn't doing anything but if I did I wasn't gonna tell him so that would be another issue.

"No I don't have any condoms Raheem will you just please go?"

"Nah I gotta feel what you been keeping from me. Don't you know I miss you girl? You cant keep running from me. You belong to me."

"So you just gonna take my stuff? Basically rape me?"

"I can't take what already belongs to me."

He started to try to climb up on top of me on the bed and I said, "You gon wake up my baby lets get on the floor."

He said "ok." When I laid on the floor on my back I realized he was still holding my shirt and I started thinking if he turns my shirt a loose I can get away. As he started to lay on top of me I said, "You're too heavy and I cant breathe, let me turn around on my hands and knees."

He said, "ok."

I got on my hands and knees and he was still holding my shirt and struggling to take his shoes off. I lifted my shirt off and got back on my hands. He didn't have anything to hold onto now because he had already torn my panties off. I was butt naked on the floor shaking and desperately thinking of a way out before this man could rape me.

He was trying to put himself inside me, trying to hold his sweater under his chin and keep me on the floor by holding my waist. His sweater kept falling down so he started to lift it over his head. In that split second when he took his hands off me I jumped up and ran out the door screaming into my moms room. I turned the light on and picked up the phone and called 911. My mom jumped up and asked what was going on. I told her Raheem had broken into the house and was trying to rape me. By now the whole house was up…my nieces and my sister had all come running in the room. My mom went in the bedroom where Raheem was trying to put back on his shoes.

She said, "What the fuck you doing in my house?"

He said, "I love her."

She said, "ok mutherfucker, uma show you love."

She went and got her gun out the closet. His pants were falling down and he started tripping and stumbling trying to get down the stairs and get out of the house.

My sister grabbed my mom and tried to hold her back but she broke loose and chase behind him out the door.

"911 whats your emergency?"

"My son's father just broke into my moms house and tried to rape me. I have a restraining order on him. Pop, pop, pop! Oh shit!"

"Ma'am is that gun fire?"

"Yes!!! Oh my God my mom is shooting at him."

"Ma'am we have officers on the way. Please don't leave your house. I have you at 1900 Whitehall Forest?"

"Yes ma'am. Please send somebody quick my mom is going to kill him."

Then I heard three more shots go off pop, pop, pop! My momma wasn't having that shit! My sister said she's gonna kill that boy. My momma said, "You damn right!"

By now the authorities had arrived at mom's house and she knew the protocol. She had placed her gun on the coffee table unloaded with the extra bullets lying on the coffee table. When they entered the apartment they started asking me a lot of questions about what happened and I just told them everything. I was tired. Tired of Raheem having me live in fear. I wanted him to pay for everything he had done to me. I know if they didn't lock him up he wasn't gonna stop until he erased me from the world. It was in that moment I realized he was never gonna leave me alone and let me be happy. So I knew I was gonna have to kill him. The days went by and I made up my mind what I was gonna do. I thought about it long and hard. I didn't want to take him away from his family and kids but it was obvious that he didn't give a damn about taking me away from mine. I knew he drank heavily and whenever he made it home after drinking he fumbled with his keys and he staggered a lot. So late one night after I new he was at the club I got dressed in a black sweatsuit, skull cap and gloves. I drove to his neighborhood and parked my car two streets over from where he lived. I had a bottle of lighter fluid and a cigarette lighter with me. I walked to his house and squirted the whole bottle of lighter fluid all on his porch and sidewalk in a trail leading into the grass where I was hiding.

My plan was to light the grass once he started trying to unlock his door and watch his ass go up in flames! I was then gonna change out of the clothes I had on and put them in separate trash bags and throw them in different dumpsters on the way back home. I laid out there for hours thinking of how he was gonna be screaming and running around on fire. I laid out there for hours waiting for his ass to come home and soon I noticed the sky was showing signs of the sun coming up very soon. He never came home that night. That had to be God watching out for him because I was serious as a heart attack about my intentions of killing him. And watching out for me because my ass prolly would've ended up in prison.

Even though I had it all planned out in my head how it was gonna go, it could've went a whole other way. I prolly watch too much damn tv. I don't know how I thought I was gonna get away with that. I was just so tired of him fucking with me and I wanted it to be all over. It wasn't long after that I was notified he had court. I found out they were trying to give him 50 years for rape. I was in disbelief! I didn't feel like he should be locked up for that long because technically he hadn't rape me because I got away from him but I knew he needed to be off the streets and given the help he needed to be rehabilitated….but at the same time how was that my issue and why in the hell after all he had done to me should I care about what happened to him? Because in my mind I still had to play fair and do the "right thing."

I lived by a different set of codes that many say they do but don't truly honor. There are certain codes that the streets live by that the average person doesn't. That code is unspoken yet well known. You keep your mouth shut and don't put the white people in your business. You didn't see nothing, you didn't hear nothing, you don't know nothing, you don't remember nothing. Not just for a situation like this but for anything street related…..fights, shootings, robberies, murders or drug deals gone bad…you don't know nothing about it even if you witnessed it because that meant you were a snitch….and snitches get stitches and end up in ditches. Plus you would be labeled a rat….and no one wanted that title. Ain't that the dumbest shit? So regardless of what he had done to me and regardless of the fact that I needed the help of the police at the time, my hood status un-spokenly said I was suppose to remain silent and remember nothing so I wouldn't be responsible for this man getting 50 years in prison even though technically I wasn't responsible for what could happen to him through the courts because he had violated me. And that's just what my stupid ass did. Remained silent.

My mom and I had been subpoenaed to appear in court to testify about what happened the night Raheem had broken into my mom's house. I wasn't there when the Marshall's brought the subpoena to my mom's house but they left it with her. I didn't answer to the summons because I'd been advised by Raheem's lawyer that if they didn't put the subpoena in my hands then technically I hadn't been served. When it was time to appear in court my mom went but I didn't. I followed his lawyer's advice and didn't show up. Evidently the judge wanted him bad because of his prior offense toward me because she sent the police back to my mom's house looking for me. The state prosecutor had called my phone several times and I lied to them saying that I would be in court. This foolish behavior took place for a couple of days where I didn't show up for court.

When the Deputy Sheriff came by my job is when shit started to get real. I wasn't at work but they left a message with my supervisor. She called me and said you better show up in court because they are threatening to take your kids away from you if you don't. I was scared to death of the possibility of my kids being taken from me. I called the judges chamber and told her aid that I would be in court in the morning. But by now the judge had gotten tired of my shenanigans and told her aid to let me know if I didn't show up to court the next day she was going to issue a bench warrant for my arrest for failure to appear.

I've never been arrested, never been in handcuffs (by the law lol) so I didn't have any plans on seeing what it was like. So my ass was in court the following morning at 9:00 am. Before court began the judge called me to her chambers. She wanted to know what had kept me from coming to court up to now….was I being threatened by the perpetrator? I told her no I hadn't been threatened…...I was just scared, I've never been in a situation like this before…. I didn't know what to do so I ran. She reassured me that I was in good hands and I was safe to tell my side of the events that took place on the night that police were called to my moms residence. I told her ok. Once inside to courtroom the prosecution began to give detailed accounts of the 911 called placed by me on the night in question. They played the entire recorded conversation. Then they began to question me.

THEN GOD MADE HIM

As I listened to my very own voice in a frantic plea for help. I remembered the fear I felt in that moment. I recalled the terror that held me. I told them that I had taken a sleep aid on that night and I didn't remember what had happened. Can you believe I actually said that? The prosecutor said judge Your Honor it so obvious the witness is terrified to testify against this narcissist. We have the recorded conversation of her plea for help and the sound of the gunshots fired by her mother in efforts to protect her. She even identified him as her sons father Raheem Shaw in that call. What more proof do we need pursue charges? He violated the standing TPO so clearly he has no respect for authority or the laws of this State. If we don't do something today there may not be a next time. I don't want that blood on my hands. After what seemed like hours of back and forth deliberation I was allowed to leave. I felt like a weight had been lifted off me after all the ducking and dodging I had done still trying to save my abuser…silly me. He went to prison for four years.

A few months later I found the love of my life….Jamel. He was everything I was missing. He was a hard working man, he was good to me and my children and he never said a harsh word to me. He stayed about 4 doors down from my mom and I had basically started staying the night down there with him a couple times a week after I made sure Nandi and lil Raheem were asleep and their school clothes were ready for the next day. One particular night around 11:00 pm Jamel ask me "Why do we always leave the kids at your moms house?"

"Because that's the best place for them."

He said, "No the best place for them is here with us so get up and let's go get them."

"My mom is going to be so mad."

"So what them your children and we going to get them now so get up and put on your coat and let 's go."

It was so cold outside and that walk seemed like it took

forever and it was only about 500 feet between our houses. When we got to my moms house and I started putting their coats on over their pajamas my mom asked me where did I think I was taking them out in this cold this time of night. I said they're going with me, she said why I said because they belong with me. I picked up Nandi and handed her to Jamel and then I picked up my baby and we left. When we got to his house we put them in our bed and I said "now where are we going to sleep?" He said "I'm gonna make us a pallet on the floor". My kids were smiling as they drifted back off to sleep. I knew then he was the one.

Any man that cares abut your kids has to care about you. Life was good! Jamel was younger than me but he had an old soul. He knew the streets but was far from a street dude. That was fine with me. I absolutely loved the fact that he got up and went to work every day just like me. It was a new love, an effortless love. A kind, gentle, almost primal love. We couldn't keep our hands off each other. It was going down anywhere and everywhere. Raheem was in prison and I wasn't scared for the first time in a long time. For the longest I felt like I had been holding my breath for a lifetime and now I could finally breathe. He talked to me even though he didn't ask a lot of questions. He made me aware that he absolutely loved me, and I felt it in the way he looked at me, the way he spoke to me, and the way he touched me.

He never spoke about my situation with Raheem, he just listened whenever I chose to speak on it. One day we were at home in our new apartment watching What's Love Got To Do With It, the Tina and Ike Turner movie, the scene where Ike grabbed Tina over the sofa and pulled her down the hall by her hair while she was kicking and screaming. It was a little too much for me to bear so I got up off the sofa and went into our bedroom. I sat on the bed with my head hanging down and began to cry as I recalled being pulled down the hallway by my hair by Raheem. I was overcome with emotions that I thought I'd forgotten about. A few moments later Jamel came into the room and closed the door. He walked over and stood in front of me, lifted my head up by my chin and wiped my tears away with his thumb. He kissed my eyelids and said softly to me almost in a whisper… "I will never hurt you. I will never put my hands on you to hurt you. I love you and that is your past and we are your future." I believed him. He kissed me and just held me and let me cry in his arms. It was so comforting. In this present time I am reminded of a moment in our life together.

Valentine's Day was in a day or so away and we were broke. I wanted to get Jamel something but I didn't have the money. We said that we weren't gonna exchange gifts because we were both strapped for cash but I still wanted to get him something because he meant so much to me and giving him a small token to express that wasn't asking too much. Besides, Valentine's Day was for lover's and people in love and we were definitely lovers and in love. It just wasn't in our budget to buy gifts this year and it bothered me. I did plan on cooking him a really nice meal and doing all things extra freaky with him that night. I woke up on Valentine's Day morning and went to the bathroom to pee. I hadn't turned the lights on until I got up to wash my hands. When I did I saw that the mirror was covered in red lipstick with the words I Love You, I Love You, I Love

You written at least a hundred times and a single red rose from the gas station sat on the sink. I was standing there with my mouth hanging open thinking this was the sweetest gesture of love anybody had given me ever! It was the simplest thing but meant the world to me, more than all the expensive jewelry, clothes and trips I had been given. I went back into our bedroom with intentions on waking him up in the best way to tell him thank you but he was laying there looking at me smiling and the only thing I could see clearly was his pretty white teeth shining even in the darkness of the room. I kissed him and said "baby that's the sweetest and best gift you could have ever given me. It means more to me than you'll ever know." He said,"I just had to do something for you." I remember being asleep one time and I felt Jamel kissing me. He was planting small kisses on my eyelids my forehead and face and in between each kiss he kept saying softly "I love you….I love you." I started to open my eyes but I just continued to play sleep because I thought if I let him know I was awake he would stop. So I kept my eyes closed and just soaked up all that love he was giving me.

I don't think no one, not a single person has ever professed his love for me in a more heart felt, heart melting, sorrowfully blissful way that he did that night. As much as he did sweet things for me he also did aggravating things to me that I loved just the same like pouring cold water on me while I was in a hot shower or pinning me down on the floor while he licked my face all over and laughed as I screamed and tried to wiggle out of his grasp until I laughed while telling him his breath stinks. Jamel loved me like a child…. innocently. I felt it deep down in my soul…...the place where Jesus lives. I got pregnant and I was excited about it but it was short lived. I left work one day to go have an ultrasound to determine just how far along I was and after it was over the doctor told to me I needed to head straight to the emergency room and she would meet me there but she didn't say exactly why. I told her I needed to go home and make sure my kids were ok first and she said no go directly to the ER. I said ok. I went straight home took a shower, made sure my kids were good and waited for Jamel to come home so he could go with me.

We got to the hospital about and hour and a half later. I gave them my name and they said they were expecting me. They put me in an exam room and told me to get completely undressed and put on the gown that was on the bed for me. I did and Jamel asked me why did they have me coming down here and not let me know what was going on? I told him I was just as puzzled. I told him I had to go to the bathroom, it was right outside of my room down the hall. As I was peeing I heard this sound that was like a loud pop but inside my stomach. As I wiped myself I felt this sharp pain and it felt like my stomach was about to buss open. I stood up and immediately doubled over in pain. I screamed for Jamel and started crying. I didn't know what was happening. Jamel came into the bathroom and pulled me in his arms as I was crying and carried me back to the examination room laid me on the bed and went to get the nurse. When they came back into the room I was tossing and turning from side to side begging for help. The doctor was called and I was rushed into emergency surgery. While they were wheeling me down the hall on the gurney I was removing my earrings and necklace handing it to Jamel.

The doctor was explaining that I had an ectopic pregnancy and was six weeks pregnant. The baby had started developing and growing in my fallopian tubes and not my uterus. Because it was stuck in my tube and didn't have enough room to grow it burst the tube and caused an accumulation of about 2 cups of blood in my stomach that could have easily resulted in my death. They new it was a life threatening situation and they had to take action immediately when I came for my office visit but they couldn't tell me at the time because they didn't have all the details and didn't want to scare me with their assumptions which is why I was suppose to go to the emergency room from her office.

This would be my fourth major surgery on my abdomen. A gunshot wound to my stomach when I was 16 years old and two cesarean births. Once the surgery was over I was left with one fallopian tube. Jamel was with me at the hospital everyday. He would get off work and come there, take a shower in my room and get in the bed with me. Once I was released I went home with him and he took care of me. He bathed me and changed my pads, gave me my medicine and made sure I ate and he checked on my children that stayed with my mom until I got better. I've never had anyone to care for me so intimately. I thanked God for him. I started to heal and things got back to normal. We pretty much couldn't keep our hands off each other. Needless to say a year later I was pregnant again. I couldn't believe it! He was ecstatic and I didn't want a baby. I told him I was going to have an abortion and he begged me not to. He was crying, snot was coming out of his nose and I was crying and saying I didn't want to go through this again because it was too hard. He said that he would always be there for me and I wouldn't have to do it all on my own. I was scared but he convinced me to keep the baby.

Eight months later Jada Simone was delivered early, a day after Christmas 2003. This was the fifth major surgery on my stomach. She was beautiful but not at first. You know everybody thinks their baby is pretty. She was long red and mean looking. She was a light skinned girl version of her dad. She was born premature but as the days and weeks went on she developed into the most beautiful baby I'd ever seen. Jamel use to always say "thank you for my baby Skye, she is so pretty!" He loved that lil baby and he loved us. It wasn't a perfect relationship by no means, nobody's relationship is. We had a few disagreements, arguments and indiscretions but that's my business.

At the end and the beginning of the day Jamel was loyal and that mattered more than any problems we may have encountered. Raheem was in prison and wanted to know if it was ok for him to call and talk with his son from time to time. Jamel and I decided together that it would be ok. Raheem called the house to speak to his son one night around 9:30 pm. When Jamel answered the phone I heard him saying "hey man don't ever call my house this late talking about you want to speak to your son. He has school in the morning and is in the bed asleep and it ain't nothing you need to talk to my lady about. So for future reference if you want to talk to your son you gon have to call at a more reasonable time"….and he hung up the phone. He handled that and I was glad he didn't feel the need to check with me about what he said. He did what any man should do when he is the head of his household, he ran it.

Time went on and we kept maintaining. June 17th 2005, would be known to me as one of the worst days of my life. Jamel was killed. My whole world was crushed. I didn't know how to believe it. I was devastated. I was angry at God. I didn't understand why he took Jamel, the one who had shown me love….and left Raheem, the one who showed me nothing but pain. I felt it should've been Raheem instead of Jamel. It just didn't seem fair in my opinion. Raheem called me a few days later and asked me what size mattress I had. I asked him why because it didn't make sense for him to ask me that. He said "so I'll know what size sheets to buy for the bed when I get home."

In his true nature he was exactly who he has always been and always will be….Satan's spawn. It would've been too much like right for him to just say I'm sorry you lost your baby's father. He was pure evil and I hated him. I HATED HIM! Three months later he was released from prison and almost immediately he started to harass me. I allowed my son to spend time with him I just didn't allow him to come to my apartment. I didn't want him to know where I lived. Other than the occasional phone call when he was drunk or him telling me I'm gonna help him get some money or else, I really tried to ignore him and not wish bad things for him. I still never trusted him and didn't want anything to do with him. The day after Christmas of that same year the kids and I had been celebrating Jada's 2nd birthday with family and friends. Nandi stayed the night with her cousins while lil Raheem and Jada came home with me.

Everybody got settled and feel asleep. Hours later I heard this explosive sound at the door that awakened me and the kids. I looked out my bedroom window and it was Raheem trying to kick the door in. I got up and immediately put a chair under the front doorknob in hopes that it would keep him from getting in. My son asked me who was that. I told him it was his dad. He started crying and asked me why was daddy trying to kick in the door. I told him I didn't know. I called the police and told them what was happening. The 911 Operator heard the noise and asked me if that was him kicking the door and I said yes. She asked me if I could give a physical description of him and I did. She told me to stay calm and don't worry we have a patrol car in your area and he should be there any minute now and that she would stay on the phone with me until he arrived.

Moments later the kicking stopped. I thought he had left. About 5 to 10 minutes later there was a knock at the door and it was the police. I opened the door and the police told me that they had a person in custody in the car and could I come to identify if it's the same person that was kicking at my door. He showed me the footprint that was embedded in the door. We walked back down to his patrol car and I let the officer know that it was Raheem. He said that he was just walking down the sidewalk when he pulled up and he fit the description that I had given the dispatcher. They locked him up for disorderly conduct. Some girl that he was messing with called my cell phone a little while later and asked me was I going to press charges. I told her yes. She asked me not to because he had just gotten out of prison and he wasn't going to hurt me he just wanted to drop our son's Christmas gifts off to me. I told her if he wanted to drop off gifts he should've taken them to his mom's house or to my mom and I could've picked them up. I didn't know he knew where I lived. I told her if that was the case why was he trying to kick in my door, he never knocked and it was after 3 o'clock in the morning when he did it. I told her she didn't know him like I did and please don't ever call me again trying to vouch for his actions.

I know all too well what he was capable of doing when he kicked in my door before. I hung up the phone. I was so scared and frazzled that I was shaking as they pulled off in the patrol car. There were several people standing outside and the courtesy officer was there as well. He walked me back to my apartment and I asked him if he didn't mind could he stay there with me and my kids because I was really shook. I knew it was out of the norm to ask him that but I was relieved when he said he would stay. He sat on in the chair as I hugged my son and rocked him back to sleep the baby never woke up during the commotion. I was grateful. I don't think either one of us slept that night. The next morning after I let the courtesy officer out I started preparing for what I had to do. I was going to take out a restraining order against Raheem after I dropped my son off to my mom. I took the deposition from the court case we had from when Raheem went to prison for assaulting me so that I would have something that the judge could reference to show that Raheem had been in trouble for putting his hands on me.

Once the judge called my name and he listened what I had to say about what had happened the night before, he told me that he wouldn't grant me a restraining order because Raheem hadn't assaulted me. I told him he had only been out of prison three months for assaulting me and was just arrested for trying to kick my door in and if he had succeeded that he would've assaulted me again. Surely he wasn't trying to kick in the door to talk to me. I gave him the document and he looked through it but said he wasn't giving me a restraining order. I started crying because I felt there was nothing I could do and I didn't even have protection from the law. I told the judge that

Raheem didn't get a chance to finish what he started four years ago, and I wasn't carried out in a body bag. I'll be prepared do defend myself if a next time comes and they'll be carrying him out in a body bag. I went downstairs to the second floor, got fingerprinted and applied for a gun permit. I was going to defend myself at whatever cost. The next day I went to purchased a firearm. I never had a reason to carry a weapon, could never see myself shooting anyone, but because I wanted to live, I found myself doing what I had to do to survive. I was tired of being scared. Time passed and I didn't have any further encounters with Raheem that were violent. I didn't put pressure on him to take care of his son financially. He provided what he wanted, God made provision for everything else.

Time passed and I moved from my apartment into my first home to start a new life. Everything was going as it should. My kids were happy and so excited about their new home. God was all up and through there. Even with me struggling and robbing Peter to pay Paul, we were making it. I was thriving and learning how to breathe….learning how to grieve the love of my life's death because I had to. My kids needed me more than I could afford to give up. Just as sure as grits is grocery…God made a way. I was happy. I wasn't trying to convince anyone of my worth. Just getting a good night's sleep and not worrying if my door was going to get kicked in meant the world to me. I still have days when the devil tries to creep into my thoughts to remind me that I was afraid, I was angry, and nobody was going to want me because I had three children by three different men. I wrestled with this off and on for some time but I was always reminded that he who angers you controls you. I truly had to let it go.

I had no more room to be angry. I'd accepted and owned up to the role I played in my abuse and I learned how to pray for him that persecuted me. I stayed in an abusive relationship far too long because I thought I could convince my abuser that I was enough and I was very afraid of him. God had not given me a spirit of fear but in my humanness, my weakness and my flesh I experienced fear because I thought I could fix it and I couldn't. God is the fixer. I'm so glad God never once took His hand off me. I'm grateful for everything…..everything! Bless up!

ABOUT THE AUTHOR

Shima Howard was born in Atlanta Ga. She had a 17-year tenor with the Ga Dept of Juvenile Justice. She has written several short stories, poems, and ghostwritten urban scripts for clients. She is the mother of Niambi H., Jameria P. and Rico S. Jr.(#forever22) and the grandmother to Ahilan P. She resides in Decatur, Ga, is retired, and is working on her next novel. God grant me the serenity to accept the things I can not change, the courage to change the things I can, and the wisdom to know the difference.

Made in the USA
Columbia, SC
06 August 2025

3dfa95cb-2639-4e4f-a25e-e1c9abefdfc3R01